Double-Cross Ranch

Double-Cross Ranch

STUART BROCK

Sagebrush
Large Print Westerns

Library of Congress Cataloging in Publication Data
Library of Congress CIP data was not provided in time for
publication. Please call (8oo) 251-8726 in the U.S. or (603)
772-1175 from Canada and we will fax or send you the
information.

Cataloguing in Publication data is available from
the British Library and the National Library of Australia.

Sagebrush Large Print Westerns are published in the
United States and Canada by Thomas T. Beeler, *Publisher,*
Box 659, Hampton Falls, New Hampshire 03844-0659.
ISBN 1-57490-236-9

Published in the United Kingdom, Eire, and the Republic of
South Africa by Isis Publishing Ltd, 7 Centremead, Osney
Mead, Oxford OX2 0ES England. ISBN 0-7531-6134 6

Published in Australia and New Zealand by Australian
Large Print Audio & Video Pty Ltd, 17 Mohr Street,
Tullamarine, Victoria, 3043, Australia. ISBN 1-86340-357 9

Manufactured in the United States of America by Sheridan
Books in Chelsea, Michigan.

CHAPTER 1

RICK MARLIN RODE HIS SKITTISH BAY OFF THE LITTLE cable ferry and into the deep shadow of the willows bordering the river. He waited there until Pancho Zapillo joined him. Pancho was barely visible on his stocky pinto with the old man lying limply across his lap.

"If what this John Amos said before he fainted is true," Rick said, "Sid Cutter and his crew ought to be in the saloon by now. Get the old fellow to the doctor and stick with him, Pancho."

"*Si*" Pancho spoke in Spanish for the sake of caution. "If we are right and they think they trailed us into town, we have the chance."

Rick's voice showed the strain of the preceding months. "If we haven't, we make the chance. I don't get chased all the way from Arizona to fail now. I'm going to find Miles. If I don't show up in a few days, you contact him. The way this old man seemed to feel, he'd be glad to hide you from Sid Cutter until hell freezes."

Pancho lifted a hand. In the darkness their eyes met. Each knew what the other was thinking: this was the end of the trail. From here on, there could be no turning back.

"*Adios*," Pancho said, and rode out of shadow into the faint light coming from the town of Riverbend, spread out at the top of the slope. Rick stayed where he was, waiting to hear if Pancho had succeeded in slipping into town without being spotted.

On the short ride across the Columbia River they had planned it this way. Since Sid and his men had not yet

1

had a chance to learn that Pancho had joined Rick in Oregon, Pancho was the one with the best chance of getting the old man to the doctor. If he managed to get into town without rousing a possible lookout, then Rick could risk going to find Miles Owen. If not, Rick would have to ride away from Riverbend and seek another way in.

He waited with characteristic patience, counting the passing seconds automatically. When they had added to five minutes and he had heard no alarm, he reined the bay onto the road leading to the ferry dock and started up the short slope toward town.

The only lights were those over the hotel and the two saloons. Rick glanced briefly up the two-block-long main street, remembering that John Amos had said Sid Cutter hung out at the River Bar—the larger saloon across from the hotel.

Seeing no one, Rick swung into full view, crossed the street, and found, as he had hoped, an alley running behind a dark livery barn. He followed the alley cautiously, recalling how Sid had almost trapped him in one back in Arizona.

Halfway up the first block he cut through a vacant lot to another street and paused there in the shadow of a wide-branched pine. The street seemed empty of life, with none of the solid, frame homes showing a light.

Rick proceeded up the street, following directions given him casually in some of Nan Owen's letters. She had written—mailing her letters from Spokane Falls to his Tucson bank for the sake of safety—that Miles had the biggest house in Riverbend. ". . . as you'd expect, Rick. And it's of brick, the only one. Isn't that typical of Dad? To buy the best he can afford and live as high off the hog as he can while he has the money. Of course,

2

the brick house doesn't mean much now except that a year ago he could afford it. He still could—and a dozen more—if he hadn't given help to so many when he was busy founding this town. But that's Dad's way, isn't it? He's even honest about his little dishonesties."

That was a thumbnail sketch of Miles, Rick thought, remembering that letter—now over a year old. And he couldn't help wondering what had happened in the meantime to change things so when they had been running as smoothly as a man could expect from life.

At first when that crew of strangers had struck at the Lazy M down in Arizona, Rick and Pancho had taken them for rustlers. But they had hit only the Lazy M of all the ranches around. And after they had cleaned the range, they had kept on hitting. Rick realized now that the attacks on the ranch itself, the burning, even the wanton killing of Pancho's sister and her husband, had been for more than the desire for money.

And the only answer he could find was revenge against Miles. Yet that was hard to believe. Few people knew that Miles still owned the Lazy H. And few in Arizona even knew that Miles was still alive. With the old murder charge hanging over Miles, Rick had always been careful in sending up the profits—making the two-hundred-mile trek to Tucson to transact that business. And certainly no one but Pancho and he could know that Miles Owen of Riverbend, Washington Territory, was Miles O. Parker, five years out of Arizona with a price still on his head.

But the attack on Miles was the only answer; an attack that had destroyed the Lazy M, forced Rick into killing a man, and had sent him running from Arizona with both the strange crew and the law at his heels. He hadn't been running from danger but to warn Miles..

3

Nor was he coming to Miles to cry for help, but to offer the only things he had left to offer: his strength and his gun.

Pancho felt the same, Rick knew. But in Pancho the anger lay closer to the surface. And more than once since he and Pancho had made rendezvous in eastern Oregon, he had had to hold the slender Mexican from turning to ambush their pursuers. It was hard for Pancho to be patient when he could almost reach out and touch the men who had deliberately burned to death his sister and her husband.

Bit by bit, Rick saw it all a little more clearly. There was Nan's telegram, waiting for him when he had risked going to Tucson to draw out what money there was in the bank. Before the attack he might have regarded the telegram as coming from an imaginative child—despite the fact that Nan was no longer the sixteen-year-old tomboy he had said goodbye to, but a twenty-one-year-old lady. Her words were the first proof that the attack was directed at Miles and not just the ranch itself.

NEED HELP. AM DOING THIS WITHOUT PERMISSION.

She had sent it in Spanish.

Miles would never ask help of any man, not even one as close to him as Rick.

Bit by bit, Rick thought. First the attack and then the clever maneuver that had forced him and Pancho into gunplay. After that, the telegram and the pursuit that looked as if Sid and his outfit were giving Rick his head and trailing him rather than trying to catch him. As if it had all been planned in advance by a capable general.

And then there was the old ferryman, John Amos. A half hour after Rick and Pancho had watched Sid and his crew cross the river, they had ridden down to the ferry to find the old man lying in his own blood and

4

unconscious. Rick had brought him to.

The old man's voice had shown surprising strength as he blinked up at the two men. "I asked for a dollar a head, man and beast," he said in a querulous tone, "and got beat with a gun butt. That's Sid Cutter—saloon sweepings."

Rick asked for more information while he bandaged the old man with what materials he had on hand. He learned that Sid had ridden out of Riverbend the previous fall and had not returned until tonight. And he learned that before getting off the ferry, Sid had asked if the old man had seen a tall young cowboy, burned dark and wearing his hair long like an Indian.

"That's you," the old man observed.

"Did he ask about anyone else?"

"Nope." And Rick knew that they weren't aware that Pancho had met him in Oregon. Then the old man said, "Even if I'd seen you before, bedamned to Sid Cutter. The way I see it, any man he's on the prowl for can't have much wrong with him."

"What of the law?" Rick demanded. "You can have him picked up, can't you?"

"The law!" For all his pain the old man managed a sharp laugh. "He'll be buying drinks for the law right now or I'm not John Amos."

Amos had managed to show Rick the simple controls of the ferry and to give directions to the doctor's house and then he had sagged back into unconsciousness.

Rick rode on up the silent street, the hoofs of the bay muffled in the soft dust of late summer. He crossed one street and went to where another came in before he saw the brick house. It was at the north edge of town, almost against the timber that pressed down from that direction.

Rick rode around the north side and beyond it until he

5

came to a carriage shed fronting on the alley. He slipped the bay into deep shadow and eased from the saddle. Between him and the house was an open space of dry-looking lawn. He walked softly toward the dark building. He had an urge to hurry, now that he was so near his goal, but he held back, knowing that even now Sid Cutter could have planned a trap for him to step into.

He reached a corner and paused to listen, his feet sinking into the soft, floury dirt. He took one more step and then drew back sharply. He had almost run into a man who stood silently beneath a low, wide window.

Rick could make out no more than that the man was working with some kind of instrument. In a moment the window swung open and the man grunted and turned, giving a soft, low whistle.

A few seconds later a taller man stepped from a hedge of low bushes that ran along some twenty feet from the house.

"That rider go on?" It was the man by the window. His voice was pitched high and whining.

"Turned down the alley," the other said. "I think this is craziness."

"Think we'll ever get a better chance? Owen don't leave town very often."

"It ain't our job to do all the dirty work," the tall man complained.

"You're getting paid, ain't you? Shut up and give me a boost."

The taller man swore softly and then cupped his hands and held them for the other to use as a step. With a grunt, he lifted a leg, put one hand on the window sill, and prepared to heave himself up.

Rick drew his gun and stepped around the corner.

"That'll be all, gents. Raise your hands."

There was the gasp of sudden shock and the taller man jumped back, spun and reached for his own gun. Rick closed in quickly. His rush knocked the tall man sideways, driving him against the side of the house. The man at the window dropped to the soft dirt, caught himself, and charged head down. Rick stepped aside, slashing down with his gun barrel. The man kept going forward, staggering until he collapsed nose down in a flower bed. He lay motionless.

Turning, Rick saw that the first man had caught his breath and was coming at him. Lashing out with his foot, Rick caught the man's gun wrist, sending the gun dropping free. They moved together, Rick swinging to knock the other out, the tall man seeking a hold on his weapon. He got it as Rick struck him. Rick's rush knocked the man into a sitting position. He stayed there, holding his gun in both hands, and aimed at Rick's middle. Rick got a big hand on his gun wrist again and gave a bone-cracking wrench. The man sobbed in pain as the wrist gave. There was a sharp, hard sound as the gun went off.

It took Rick a moment to realize that the man had pulled the trigger the instant his wrist had given way— and had shot himself.

There was a questioning whoop from up the street. It was answered from the alley; then Rick caught the sound of hoofs pounding from two directions.

He broke for the alley and his horse. The sounds of riders were sweeping closer, coming from the alley and the street northward, pincering him.

This town sleeps light, he thought bitterly as he swung into the saddle.

He headed the bay north, driving his heels heavily

into its flanks. His start was a matter of yards, his advantage the darkness. He broke from town and onto the open prairie and from there into a stretch of timber.

He was a range-country man and he did not know how to cope with the sudden savage closing in of the forest. Branches reached from darkness to slap him, ripping at his flat-crowned hat and his clothing, making the bay more skittish than ever. Rick could hear the thrashing behind him as his pursuers turned too, led by the noise of his passage. He kicked almost savagely at the bay, seeking speed, flattening himself as much as possible. Belatedly he realized his mistake. Thick timber was hardly the element for a southern border man.

A clearing loomed ahead and the bay picked up speed again. But then it was gone and there was timber again. What had looked like sanctuary at first now had the appearance of a trap. Rick drew to a halt at the edge of the trees and chanced a look behind.

They came into the clearing, single file, a dozen riders, heading straight for where he sat. He jerked the bay about and once more slashed his way into the heavy darkness of the forest. He kept working to his left, hoping he could strike the river and follow it back to town and perhaps to Miles' house. If he could shake them completely, he figured it would be safe enough to use Miles' place as a hideout.

But the timber betrayed him completely. It ran almost to the river as he had hoped, but it turned into swampland beneath the bay's driving hoofs. One minute they were on solid ground, the next Rick felt the horse flounder fetlock deep in marsh, grunting and straining at the clinging mud, at footing too soft for swift going.

Rick could hear them closing in now, led unerringly

8

by his blundering passage through the trees and underbrush. Grimly, he urged on the pony. Then he heard a shot, not thirty feet behind, and knew they had caught up.

He did not hear the bullet but it brought a sudden flash of fire along his left side, driving him nearly from the saddle. He sat a moment after regaining his balance. Then he heard a bull-voiced cry:

"Alive, you fools!"

There were no more shots.

Rick made an effort to rein in the bay now, hoping to sit quietly and let his pursuers flounder around in the swamp. But the unfamiliar surroundings had completely spooked the horse and when he felt the bit dig at his mouth, he snorted and plunged forward, pawing wildly for hard, dry ground.

"Dead ahead!" the bull-like voice cried out exultantly.

Rick drew his gun, ready to fire. He stopped, easing down the hammer as he clung to the jolting bay with his knees. The fact that they wanted him alive was a slim chance for safety that his own shooting could destroy.

Before he could holster the gun again, the bay gave a lurch, struck hard ground with a forefoot, and threw himself frantically ahead. Rick felt air instead of saddle leather beneath him. He landed hard, his breath jolting painfully, his teeth jammed together.

There was a neigh and the bay bolted off with a flick of heels that whispered dangerously close to his head. Rick lay where he had fallen, fighting for breath, and listening as the riders lined out after his horse, shouting position to one another, sounding as if they knew exactly what to do in this pursuit.

Slowly Rick lifted himself out of the mud and groped

9

his way to dry land. He tripped and lay belly down, and when he rose again, he realized that he no longer had his gun. He stopped, fumbled for matches, and then let his hands fall from his pockets. The chance of finding his gun in that swamp was too slim to risk losing precious time. Drawing in a deep breath, he swung at a jog trot down a narrow path that angled through the timber.

He had gone only a short distance when he felt the warmth of his blood running down from the wound in his side, sliding along his leg and into his boot. Soon his lungs began to pump for air and he moved in a staggering stride. He knew his own limit well enough. A cowman was nothing without a horse to ride.

He stopped, fell to his knees and then crawled into a nest of bushes. He lay on his belly, sucking hard for air. He could hear them coming back now, some distance away but making time in his direction. When he could sit up, he wadded his bandanna against his wound and bound the wadding tight with the sleeve ripped from his shirt. Then he lay back down, forcing himself to breathe more quietly.

They were near enough for him to hear them talking now.

"Ring this patch. He hasn't had time to get out. Come morning we'll get the rest of the posse and flush him."

"Posse!" Rick thought bitterly. Since when did a legal posse form in advance and wait for a man to appear—a man none up here supposedly knew existed?

It was obvious to Rick what had happened, Not finding a trace of him in town, Sid Cutter had figured Rick to be behind him. He might have had a man watching the ferry and given Rick time enough to get to Miles' house before closing the trap. To implicate Miles with a man on the dodge from Arizona would be just adding one more knot to the rope Rick had watched being woven around himself and Miles' Arizona ranch.

Only there was one thing wrong. Rick had heard Sid Cutter talk before and he had a voice that croaked with rust. This bull-voiced leader was someone else, someone whose voice Rick did not recognize.

But getting into the open safely was the first consideration. He wriggled forward, hunching to one side to keep his wound from breaking open again, and worked from the nest of brush into a patch of prairie grass. He drew himself cautiously to his knees and then went flat again as a rider loomed up in the blackness not a dozen feet away.

The man faded into the shadow of the timber and Rick worked his way forward as silently as possible, heading for another group of trees he could see ahead. it was an agonizing process and now and then he would stop to let a man on horseback slide by. When he reached the trees, he could hear them still around him, and he stayed low, crawling as before, feeling ahead with each forward move to make sure no crackling brush was in front, ready to betray him.

He came out at the top of a low rise and stood flattened against a lightning-struck stump and listened to the night sounds. When his breathing quieted, he could sort them out—those of the men from those of the forest animals. He grinned wearily, enjoying a momentary sense of triumph as he heard the movements of the men—they were all below him now.

He looked around, seeking to orient himself. He could make out faint light southward and knew that Riverbend lay there. To the east, while he watched, a thin line of light showed over the mountains. The sense of urgency closed over him once more and he left the

11

stump and started through the forest. Daylight was coming. What was it the bull-voiced man had said? "Come morning and we'll get the rest of the posse."

In daylight, a good-sized crew would have little trouble locating him unless he could get far away from where they now thought he was.

CHAPTER 2

BY EARLY AFTERNOON RICK KNEW THAT HE WAS about done for. The sun burned from a brassy sky, beating up from the hot earth into his face, hammering down on his unprotected head. He lay in tall, coarse grass that rippled above him with a steady, faint whisper. To the north, fifty feet away, was a tongue of cool green timber. From the south came the sounds of the posse, doubled in size now. He had slipped through a second cordon earlier in the day, but inevitably they were closing in again.

He had seen some of them and he recognized Sid Cutter and a couple of the crew that had attacked in Arizona. The bull-voiced man had almost come upon him more than once—a huge, red-bearded, redheaded man who sat a massive black horse befitting his size and authority. Rick had no idea who he might be except that he was dressed as a town man. But then so were a number of the others who, Rick guessed, were the "rest of the posse" that had been called in at daylight.

The bullet crease along his side had stopped bleeding, but the throb from it worked the length of his body. He tried to ignore the pain by worrying over the problem of the redhaired man's stake in all this. Why the other wanted him alive, why he had so obviously set up a trap

12

near Miles' house, Rick could not fathom. His mind worked on it while he rested and then rejected it for the more immediate problem of the approaching posse.

The sounds from the south were close enough now for him to catch the creaking of saddle leather and the jingling of bits. And soon he was able to make out the deep, baying voice of the leader.

"Spread out! He couldn't be far from here. Spread out!"

A man shouted something in the near distance, and then Rick heard the sound of a horse coming through the long prairie grass, The horse was joined by another and then another until he could imagine them making a swath like a crew of mowers in a hay field.

Again he glanced toward the beckoning tongue of timber. It seemed his lone hope now, but fifty feet of open land was too much to make a try at crossing—especially when a man's sap had run out.

The wind picked up a little, whipping the grasstops above his head. Rick studied them brushing across the hot blue of the sky and wondered if he might not have the strength to wriggle that last fifty feet. Any movement that he made just might be attributed to the breeze now.

Sucking air into his dust-choked lungs, he eased his long body forward. The movement caused the bullet wound to separate and he could feel warm blood along with the sharp, blinding pain. Holding his teeth tightly together, he reached out with his hands, got a grip on the strong grass roots, dug in behind with his toes, and pushed once more. He made a foot and then waited for the pain to subside.

Fifty feet. At a foot a minute, that was fifty minutes. And from the sounds, the posse was within three

13

minutes of finding him. He heard the voice of the leader again.

"Keep in line! Cover the whole field, This grass is tall enough to hide an army—look sharp!"

The rustling grew louder and closer. Rick could almost feel a shod hoof coming down on his back. It took every ounce of control to stay where he was instead of trying to leap up and run that last fifty feet.

He worked his tongue over dry lips and made another effort to pull himself along. This time he made twice the distance he had before. And then, above him, the grass tops ceased to wave and hung limply as the breeze shifted and was cut off from this prairie by timber. He could only lie still now; any movement would give him away.

Just behind him and to his left a horse nickered. Leather creaked under the man's weight. Rick pushed himself partially up with his hands and turned his head. The shock ran through him like the bite of a rattler. A horse and rider were within five feet, the man sitting squat and solid on a small sorrel. He was twisted, looking back as another of the posse called something from the far side of the field.

In a minute he would turn back—and when he did he would see his quarry almost under his nose.

Rick drew himself into a crouch, made a swivel on his toes so that he faced broadside to the horse and rider, and threw himself upward and outward.

The horse shied at the sudden movement from the apparently lifeless grass. With the rustle made by Rick's body and the grunt he gave as be moved with his last strength, the rider turned. His head came around in time to catch Rick's reaching, slashing arm. He started out of the saddle and Rick's weight, going up, drove him the

14

rest of the way. He cascaded into the grass with a grunt that knocked a warning shout into a gasping gurgle.

Then Rick found the stirrup with one toe, felt the horse jerk under him, caught the horn, and drew himself into the saddle. He got the reins with one desperate grab, saw with a quick glance that by some miracle the others in the field were still looking toward the far side, and kicked his heel savagely into the sorrel's flank.

The man on the ground found wind enough to shout. A gun barked a signal. Rick bent over the horse's neck, clinging to the horn as the animal's jolting gait drove fresh pain through his wounded side. Throwing the horse into a seesawing run, he aimed for the timber. Another bullet cut the air near him, and the thud of hoofs grew to a crescendo.

Now the forest loomed ahead. A deer track marked a break in the underbrush and Rick aimed the horse toward it. Lead snapped a small branch above his head and then he was in the timber, swallowed by it, mingled with its cool, shadowy gloom—and a bare chance of eluding them for a while longer lay ahead.

"Circle around! Cut him off!" It was the bull-voiced leader again.

Rick drove the small sorrel to give everything he had. Excitement and fear and the smell of an unfamiliar rider worked on the horse, and with ears flat it breasted the thin undergrowth that lay along the deer trail, stumbled over rotting deadfalls, and beat its way steadily up a slight incline, leaving the shouting far to the rear.

But Rick knew that before long they would catch him. Here in unfamiliar territory he was at a disadvantage. And now, as the horse followed the twisting deer trail upward, he lost all sense of direction. If the track should lead back to where he had started, he

15

wouldn't know it until too late.

With startling abruptness, the slight pitch became a steep slope, and suddenly he broke into a long, bone-bare ridge that was high enough above the surrounding timber for him to see the pattern of the countryside,

The sun told him that he was facing due south. Off to his left the trees stretched in an unbroken sea of green to distant hills. He could make out the river and the tiny spot of brown beside it that was Riverbend. Beyond it lay the desert he had crossed yesterday. Below him, he could see a ranch house and, here and there, the dark patches of groups of cattle.

It was country worth looking at—mixed timber and prairie and seemingly enough water—judged from a cowman's point of view. But there was no time to look longer as the sounds of the posse rose from below. He put heels to the sorrel, heading back into the timber.

He kept working north and a little east, cutting back here and there to avoid a gully or a too thick tangle of brush, but always getting back onto his line of flight.

Finally he found what he had been seeking—a temporary refuge. Years before a great landslide had ripped down the mountain, leaving a tangle of rotting deadfalls and tremendous rocks. On it a few saplings and bits of brush were beginning to take root. Below, the narrow track continued to twist through the forest.

Dismounting, Rick looped the reins over the saddle horn, headed the horse downtrail, and gave him a slap on the rump. The animal sprinted forward, heading home. Quickly Rick turned and made his way painfully up the rubble of the slide until he came to a cave created by two huge boulders pressing against one another. He crawled into the shelter between them and lay on his belly, his eyes glued to the trail below.

16

In a short time the riders appeared, going single file down the trail. The red-haired man was in the lead. Sid Cutter, heavy-set and dark-bearded, was directly behind him. Rick watched them slow at the slide, pick up the track of the sorrel, and go on. Before the last man was out of sight, a final horseman appeared, riding double with the man Rick had hit.

Soon they too had disappeared into the timber. Rick swallowed once more, wondered if he would ever again know the taste of water, and fell asleep.

He awoke sore and stiff, his side feeling as if a branding iron lay hotly on it. Outside the little cave the trees were blending into a mass of shadow. Slowly, Rick dragged himself into the open, rose to his feet, and started down the loose rubble toward the trail.

Twice he slipped and fell, and each time he managed to drag himself to his feet and go on. Even when he was on firmer ground, on the trail, he pitched from side to side, unable to keep his balance. Finally he fell again and lay there, resting.

When he lifted his head to study the gloom around him, what little he could see danced weirdly in front of his eyes. He rose and staggered on. His mind went back ten years and once more he was walking numberless miles across an Arizona waste, hurting from three cracked ribs that a fall from a horse had given him. Again he was a homeless fifteen-year-old, afoot and burning with fever.

Tree branches slapped at him, confusing him because in this part of Arizona there was no true timber. And then he was in flat, shadowless darkness. Ahead, beckoning him, a light danced tantalizingly like a will-o'-the-wisp. Off to the left he heard cattle stirring, and once a steer rose up in front of him and flipped itself, frightened, out of the way. The dancing light came closer, seemed to fade, and then brightened again.

Miles' light had beckoned just that way ten years before. In Rick's mind was a vague memory of having done this very thing in just the same fashion. Somehow he knew that a man named Miles, boss and crew all rolled into one, owner of the Lazy M ranch, would find him stretched in the dirt of his yard, would take him in the house, nurse him back to health, and give him a home. He knew these things with a certainty that drove him steadily toward the light.

He plunged ahead, fell, rose again, and staggered forward. He almost lost his balance as the light came close enough to be reached for with his hands, caught himself, tripped over the mountainous height of a step, and fell flat on the rough wood of a veranda floor.

Windy Litten, the lone hired hand on the DR spread, was setting new corral posts while he waited for his boss to whip up breakfast. When the red-bearded man rode up on his big black, Windy lifted a hand briefly in greeting and returned to his work.

He had managed to keep his job for three months— the longest of any DR hired man—by looking like a man interested only in his daily work. When he had drifted into Riverbend and looked around for a place to spread his soogans, he had learned that displaying any interest except in his work would lose him the DR job quickly. The previous men had all gone that way when they forgot that Dell Ryan was more than their boss, noticing that she was a young and attractive woman as well.

Besides, Windy had discovered early that prying into

the comings and goings of Ed Foley was not his job. Nor was noticing the apparent paralysis of the place, the lack of interest on the part of the owner when line shacks were burned, fence cut and, now and then, prime beef missing.

It was a pretentious-looking ranch on the surface. The house was solid, the buildings kept up, the graze well watered. But the appearance was deceptive: the grass supported less than half the beef it could handle, the outbuildings held little but air, and the house was furnished only in the parlor, kitchen, and main bedroom.

Now as Ed Foley tied his black and walked to the door, Windy kept his head down to his work, his inevitable cigarette dangling from his lips and working smoke up into his left eye. He was a short, bull-necked man who seemed neither sullen nor happy, neither dull nor curious. He looked much like any other fiddle-footed cowhand who drifted around the country.

Even so, he noticed that Ed Foley kept looking back at him while he hammered on the parlor door. When Dell Ryan opened up and Foley strode inside, he said at once:

"What's Windy hanging around out there for?"

"Because I put him to work there."

Foley took a pipe from his pocket and began to stuff it with rough-cut tobacco. "I trailed Marlin here. Did he stay?"

"A man came just before dawn," she admitted. She returned to her kitchen, letting him follow. "His name is Marlin? What is it this time, Ed?"

Dell Ryan looked to be ten years younger than Ed Foley. She was tall for a woman and yet she barely reached his shoulder. She had thick dark hair that she wore in a loose knot at the back of her finely shaped head. Her eyes were large and dark in an oval face that could be soft and feminine or hard and worldly, depending on her mood and the needs of the moment. Her mouth was wide and full, with a sensual warmth in the twist of her lips.

She was always a little nervous around Foley and now she spoke quickly, as if apologizing. "He's in bad shape. I put him to bed."

"He was pretty good sized," Foley said. "Did you get Windy to help?"

She turned meat in the frying pan. "Windy doesn't know." For a moment she sounded defiant. "Have I ever included Windy in anything, I heard your posse on the prowl. Don't you think I have any sense?"

"Sometimes," he said smoothly. He flipped up the lid of the coffee pot, sniffed, and poured himself a cup. He sat at the kitchen table, puffing his pipe and sipping the steaming coffee.

She moved impatiently. "You're always driving my hired men away, Ed. Let Windy alone. I can't run this place alone." As if encouraged by her defiance, she said swiftly, "Why can't I move to town? I'm sick of trying to pretend to be a rancher. I'm sick of pretending to be persecuted by Miles Owen."

"You can't move to town, because it isn't time yet," he said harshly. "We're too close for you to jump the traces now." There was a commanding sharpness, an arrogance, in his tone. "Roundup this fall will see us done—and the end of Owen. Remember that." He shifted his weight on the chair. "Think this fellow Marlin will live?"

"If his fever breaks soon, he'll come out of it," she said. "He's strong."

"And handsome, I hear," Foley said sourly. He got

20

up. "I want a good look at him."

She led him down a hallway and into the one furnished bedroom. It was obviously her own. Rick lay stretched out on the canopied walnut bed. He was still in his clothes except for his boots. He lay with his eyes shut, breathing raggedly. His skin where it showed beneath his beard and dirt was flushed with fever.

"Who is he?" she asked again. "What is this all about Ed?"

He drew her back to the kitchen. "Rick Marlin. He was Miles Owen's partner on a spread down in Arizona. He came here on the dodge, looking for Owen. It seems there was some sort of trouble with rustlers down there and Marlin is wanted for murder."

Dell said thoughtfully, "So that's where Sid and his outfit went last fall." She suddenly remembered her meat and rushed to lift it, smoking from the pan. Then she turned on Foley. "Go on, Ed. You haven't told me anything yet."

He shrugged. "Just that Marlin stumbled on that jackass of a town marshal and Higgins going into Owen's house. The fools let him sneak up on them." He sounded angry now. "Why do I have idiots for helpers?"

"Because you're afraid to pick anyone with brains," she retorted. "And when you do, you try to stop them from using those brains."

Foley ignored her; he had heard this before. "Marlin knocked out the marshal and shot Higgins. One of my men riding behind Owen's house heard the gun go off and raised the alarm."

Dell's smile was thin. "And just like that a posse formed. How long do you think you can fool the townspeople, Ed?"

"The townsmen weren't called until morning," Foley

21

said. "I'm not too big a fool, Dell." He finished the last of his coffee and started for the door. "I want Marlin in as good shape as possible. I'm going to undress him and wash him up now."

"Do you want him to look pretty when you hang him?"

He only laughed at her sarcasm. "He won't hang—at least, not for a while. Not until after he's helped us against Miles Owen." He laughed at the expression on her face. "Don't be surprised, Dell. That's where you come in."

He left her, then, and when he returned she had breakfast on the table. He said, "You can nurse him from here on out."

"And then what?"

Foley said smoothly, "We've got almost the whole town thinking that Owen had a hand in killing that worthless husband of yours last year. Maybe we can get Marlin thinking that Owen has changed in the five years they haven't been together—thinking that power has gone to Owen's head."

"I see what you want now," she said tonelessly. "I get Marlin in my debt—for saving his life and hiding him from the posse. Is that it?"

"That's it."

"And then I play the defenseless woman against the big frog in the swamp?"

"Get him any way you can," Foley said flatly.

Dell had no illusions. Whatever she would have to offer in exchange for Rick's loyalty, Foley would expect her to offer. Foley was not jealous, not in the regular sense of the word. He had sent her ranch hands away for more practical reasons. More than once he had told her in his scathing way that he knew her weakness

22

for young, decent-looking males and that here, in a place like Riverbend, they couldn't afford to have rumors start.

"Well?"

"What else can I do, Ed? We're in too deep to back out now."

Going to her, he put surprisingly gentle hands on her shoulders. She could see him turn on his charm and despite what she knew about him, she did not fail to respond to it as always.

Bending his head, he kissed lightly. "It won't be long before you'll have the biggest house in Riverbend. You'll have more than one ranch and you won't have to live on either of them. You can wear mink if you want."

She laughed scornfully at him. "Wear mink in Riverbend?" But even while she laughed, the old feeling, the quickened breath, the gladness at his kiss, were with her again.

"Who says we stay in Riverbend? A Territory needs political representatives, doesn't it? First to Olympia. Then who knows—to Washington, perhaps. We're on the move this time. This time we don't make mistakes. Don't you think I'm as tired of pretending to be nothing but a newspaperman as you are of running a ranch? It'll all be changed by the time roundup is over."

He drew her close to him, smiling down at her, radiating the charm that was so valuable to him. With an effort she forced herself away from him.

"Go home, Ed. Windy will want his breakfast." Then she gasped. "How can I keep him from learning about Marlin?"

Foley scratched his beard thoughtfully. "Send him out to ride fence," he said finally. "Have him go to town and pick up a couple of men and make a big job of it.

I'll see that there's enough fence to mend for a few weeks. Do it this morning."

She nodded agreement and went with Foley to the front door. He stopped, one hand on the latch. "And don't get foolish over this Marlin, Dell. Don't make any mistakes now. We can't afford them."

"Go away," she said. "I'll do it and I'll do it right. You aren't all the brains in this outfit."

Foley rode off on his big black, taking it slowly on the hour-long ride to town. As always after he had had a brush with Dell, he felt edgy. Despite the fact that they had been together seven years now—since they had run out of Montana one jump ahead of the law—he didn't trust her fully. So far she had stuck with him, awaiting that promise of marriage being fulfilled when they got in the right "position." She hadn't even balked when he had talked her into marrying Ryan so they could move out here where Ryan had inherited a ranch. She had been relieved—he thought when he had deftly got rid of Ryan in such a way that the evidence of his death pointed toward Miles Owen. Yet the feeling stayed with him that he could not trust her fully.

Ed Foley had few illusions about himself and few about Dell. He knew that his scorn of society and convention had brought him close to jail more than once. Yet his contempt for others would not let him use his sharp mind in a legitimate fashion. He was doing well with the newspaper he had established as a front for this operation, but it was not enough for him.

His hands shook a little on the reins as he thought of what was to be—what could be if they did not slip this time. Not just a newspaperman in a one-horse town, but the countryside itself would be his. The half-developed land for the working, the control of the town his for the taking and, as he had told Dell, the future spread out for a man with drive and ambition and brains: politics, moving up as the Territory developed and grew.

Dell was even more impatient than he, and this waiting, this slow maneuvering, was beginning to get on her nerves. And her weakness—the weakness he had used with profit more than once—for the gay life, the bright lights and a good-looking man to share them, he was beginning to fear again. Dell lacked the patience necessary to wait for the biggest opportunities.

As always, he had kept part of his plan from her. Now with this chance to close in on Miles Owen at roundup, he debated telling her that they had come here because he had found out who Miles Owen really was; that he had sent Sid down to wipe out the Lazy M and thus weaken Miles' finances still further; that he had taken advantage of Rick Marlin's coming here with a plan to force Rick into a position where he could be used against his friend Miles.

Foley laughed to himself as he always did when he was pleased. One by one, he was pulling the props from under Miles Owen. With the collapse of the Lazy M in Arizona, only one prop—Rick Marlin—remained. When that was destroyed, Miles would be ready for the final push. And what he had built, but had not taken advantage of, would be Ed Foley's.

Ed Foley spat contemptuously. Coming here and building the town as he had, Miles could have made a fortune. He could have controlled both the town and the country by now. If he had been fool enough to let such an opportunity slip away from him, that was no fault of Foley's.

He laughed again as he shaped his plan around Rick

25

Marlin. He had meant to angle Rick into a somewhat different corner. But this luck of having him fall into Dell's hands made it all the simpler. He shaped and reshaped the plan until he found it good. Tomorrow he would tell Dell how to proceed.

CHAPTER 3

WHEN RICK DID COME TO FULL CONSCIOUSNESS, HE found himself in a small bedroom with walls of log, peeled of bark and adzed smooth. The pictures on the walls looked strange, and the curtains at the windows looked even stranger. A fancy walnut bureau stood against one wall opposite the bed which, he noticed, was of fine walnut too. Running a hand over the coverlet, he realized that he was lying between linen and under fine quilting.

He dropped his head back to the pillow, guessing that the incongruity of log walls with curtains and walnut furnishings could only point to the presence of a woman. He was not surprised when the door opened and a woman appeared.

She looked like the room—feminine and yet sensible. She was very pretty, almost beautiful. Her warm, wide mouth was quirked in a smile as she came toward him.

He liked the way she walked. She was gracefully tall in a split riding skirt. Above it, she wore a man's heavy shirt, strained by the fullness of her figure. He lay still, his eyes on her, waiting.

"You're finally awake," she said, her voice deep and low. "I was beginning to think my nursing never would cure you." She smiled more broadly, showing him fine white teeth.

Rick scratched his palm over the roughness of his face. "I have you to thank, then?" He fingered his bristly dark beard and unkempt hair. "I must be something to see!"

"Like a dogie lost about six months," she retorted. There was a chair by the bed and she sat down. "But now you look as if you'll live."

"I feel so," he admitted. "Hungry, thirsty, and wanting a smoke."

"Can do," she said, rising. She thrust out a hand. "I'm Dell Ryan and this is my DR ranch."

Rick took her hand. It was firm and uncalloused. He hesitated briefly and then said, "Rick Marlin. And it's about all I have left—my name."

She released his hand and stepped toward the door. "I know. You're the man Ed Foley is looking for."

"Red beard? Voice like a bull?"

"That's him." She went out, closing the door after her. Rick lay quietly after determining that his money belt was still there, still filled. Whoever had stripped him down to his underwear had either missed or ignored it. One of the hired hands, maybe.

Before he could do much thinking about the situation he was in, Dell Ryan returned with a tray. Rick sat up, sniffing chicken soup and coffee hungrily. He ate as a starving man will and after a few bites found himself reluctantly pushing aside the tray. He picked up the sack of tobacco lying there and rolled a cigarette. When she lighted a match, he leaned toward her eagerly, and sucked in smoke with voracious pleasure.

He was silent, waiting for her to do the talking. When she told him he had lain there almost a week, he could not help wondering what he might have said in his delirium. He watched sharply, looking for an answer in

27

her manner.

She seemed curious, nothing more. She said, "It may not be my business but men don't often fall half-dead at my door. Nor do posses usually follow the next day, demanding to search my house."

Rick sipped his coffee. "Did you let them?"

"Ed Foley is a friend of mine," she said simply. "I let him in."

Rick blew smoke slowly. "Then he'll be coming for me."

Her eyes danced with amusement. "Hardly. A man's home may be his castle but so is a woman's bedroom. I showed him the door and told him to look—but that he'd have to pardon my underclothing scattered around." She laughed softly. "He turned beet-red and almost ran away."

"Now that I'm all right, I'll have to pull out."

"With no horse? No plan?"

"I'm wanted in these parts. What else can I do?"

She said thoughtfully, "Ed Foley said you killed Tim Higgins, the deputy marshal, when he caught you trying to break into Miles Owen's house, and that you stole a horse later. I should say you are wanted. But I still have an idea."

Rick laid down his cigarette butt and rolled another. "I thought I saw this man breaking into a house. He drew. We wrestled and his gun went off, killing him. I could never prove that, of course."

He waited for her to ask him what he had been doing at Miles' house but she seemed to accept his explanation without question.

"I could give you a job here," she said suddenly.

Rick shook his head. "I'm enough in your debt," he said. "Hiding a wanted man is a crime. There's no

28

reason why you should take a chance on getting caught now that I'm well."

She rose and picked up the tray. "What I did, I did out of selfishness," she said. "I didn't know you—and I still don't, really. If I offer you a job, it's because I have to take chances—or leave here." She went out, giving him time to think over what she had said.

In the days that followed, Rick recuperated rapidly. At the same time, he probed Dell Ryan carefully for the meaning behind her remarks. She seemed reticent at first but soon she talked quite freely. When he found that she had only one man working for her, he couldn't contain his surprise.

"There were more," she explained. "But it's hard to get men to stay. When my husband was alive . . ." She stopped and Rick could see a shadow slipping across her face.

"You mean the men have been driven off?"

"Since my husband was killed, yes."

They were seated at the dinner table. Rick waited for her to go on and when she remained silent, he carefully rolled a cigarette before he said, "You're sitting on land someone else wants, is that it?"

She nodded agreement. There was strong bitterness in her voice. "He was killed last year. He wasn't much of a man and he wanted to leave. But I made him stay. I suppose you could say I had him killed."

"And they're still pushing you?"

"Still," she admitted. "But I haven't changed my mind. If they want to get rid of me, they'll have to kill me too."

"Who is 'they'?" Rick asked quietly.

"Miles Owen," she said without expression. "His land

lies next to mine."

Rick's cigarette had gone out and he took the time to relight it. He spoke cautiously. "First I hear that I try to rob this Miles Owen's house. Now I hear he killed your husband. Who is Miles Owen?"

"He owns a good part of Riverbend," she said. "He's a big man here, a powerful man." Her dark eyes were fixed on her hands folded in her lap. "The man who wants to marry me," she added. She laughed, a brittle sound. "He can't get my land any other way—except by killing me."

"I see," Rick murmured. "If you have proof, the law will . . ."

"Proof? He's too clever a man to leave open tracks. He hides his work well."

"But surely the attitude of the townspeople . . ." Rick began again. Once more he stopped, waiting.

"A lot are against him, of course. But he founded Riverbend. A lot are in his debt, too." She stood up, clearing the table with quick, jerky motions. "He has power and he wants more. That's natural, I suppose. I can marry him—and share it. Or I can fight him."

"That's what you meant the other day, then," Rick said. He studied her, but she was busily stacking the dishes under the hand pump on the sink. "The job I'm offered is to fight Miles Owen?"

Without turning, she said, "Yes."

"And likely get killed doing it?"

Again, "Yes."

"Do I go gunning for this Owen?"

"Not openly," she said. "He doesn't fight openly."

Rick didn't believe her. Miles had saved his life and had kept him—a drifting, orphan kid—had raised and schooled him. Rick couldn't picture Miles wanting to

30

squeeze another man from his land. He couldn't see Miles fighting any way but in self-defense-and that he would do openly.

Yet she sounded sincere. Almost unbidden, the thought crossed his mind that he had not seen Miles in five years. Power can go to a man's head. He pushed away the thought, but it clung.

He said in all honesty, "I think I can help you." Just see Miles, he thought. Get the truth from Miles, and then learn who was behind her trouble. He had his debt to Miles and he had his debt to her. Perhaps he could pay them both at the same time. Wanted as he was, both here and in Arizona, he had little to look forward to but running. And if he were ever to do anything about Sid Cutter, he couldn't do it by running away.

"If I get killed," he said logically, "I'm not out much. What life I have you gave me, I reckon."

She looked at him, smiling without humor, "I reckon you're right."

The day he could sit in the saddle without feeling weak in the knees, he knew that he was ready. Dell had told him that Windy Litten was due back that night or the next morning and it was time for him to leave.

At first she suggested that he slip out on an unbranded stray she had in the corral and ride into Riverbend and let her hire him. But Rick vetoed the suggestion, pointing out that if he were recognized there, he wouldn't get as far as the ranch.

"How many people there saw you?"

He hesitated. There was Sid Cutter. Yet he couldn't tell her of Sid without exposing more of his life than he cared to at the moment. He thought of the posse. "As far as I know, none—unless it would be the man whose

31

horse I stole." He grinned wryly. "If I drift in broke and someone does think he recognizes me, I won't have much of a chance. If I drift in with money in my pocket, there'll be people on my side right off."

She stared at him, a smile quirking the corners of her mouth. "In other words, I stake you. How do I know you'll come back?"

He looked down at her. His face, shaven of its dark beard, was long and lean with the muscles and bone standing close against his taut skin. "A chance you'll have to take. But I always pay my debts. And already I owe you more than money."

She shook her head—not at him but as if to clear cobwebs from her mind. Rick was a good-looking man, tall and spare and with the grace and set of a born rider. Since he had been up and around, more than just a half-alive body in her bed, his strength had bothered her. He lacked the charm of Ed Foley, perhaps, but he had a magnetism all his own.

Sensing her mood, he took a seat on the sofa beside her. She started to rise but settled back. Then with a sudden movement she faced him. "I just want to be sure, Rick. I haven't much. I—"

"I have some," he said, thinking of his share in the money belt. "But I'll need more. I plan to ride in and buy a half-interest in this place. A property owner has advantages."

She turned this over in her mind, It seemed to her an even better plan than the one Ed Foley had outlined. She studied Rick warily, wondering what more than he had said was in his mind. So far he had played it as Ed Foley had predicted—as if he were a stranger to Miles Owen. And, she thought with faint pleasure, so far he had done exactly as she had worked it out in her own plans.

As she studied him, the wariness left her and she leaned tentatively toward him. Rick's lips curved in a gentle smile and he put his hand to the back of her head, sliding his fingers through the heavy mass of her hair, drawing her face closer. Lips parted, she let herself go to him.

After a moment, Rick released her. "This is foolishness," he said.

"I know," she murmured, and drew him close again.

CHAPTER 4

WHEN RICK HAD RIDDEN OFF ON THE UNBRANDED stray, Dell made a hurried trip to Riverbend. She went openly to the newspaper office and handed Ed Foley an advertisement to be put in the Spokane Falls newspaper.

He stood across the counter from her, a copy pencil in his big hand, nodding as she told him in swift, low words of Rick's variation on their plan.

"It will work," he decided. "Marlin had enough gold in that belt to impress a lot of people here."

"So you counted it when you undressed him," she said. Her smile was sharp. "Why did you leave the money, Ed?"

"I'm no common thief!" he answered harshly.

"Of course not. Not a common one." She saw the anger on his face and she added, "Don't lose your temper, Ed. You might ruin things."

"You're getting mighty independent, Dell."

She kept on smiling. "After all, I'm going to have a partner with money. Remember that. I won't be wholly dependent on someone else now, Ed."

He marked the counter with the copy pencil and

rubbed his finger slowly over the soft lead streaks. "So that's it. You think you're in love with this Marlin."

She had an impulse to laugh. For the first time she was seeing symptoms of true jealousy in Ed Foley. And then the desire for laughter froze as she caught a glimpse of his eyes.

"Remember, Dell," he said softly, "I don't have to use Marlin against Owen. It's just the best way, that's all. I can get rid of him if I have to—and still win."

"You wouldn't, Ed. Not now."

"And why not?" he demanded. "My guess is that Marlin is playing you for a sucker. He's going to use you for a screen. How much does he know?"

"I've watched him," she said hastily. "He's uncertain about Miles. I can see that. But he doesn't know—he doesn't suspect. I'm sure."

"And now she pleads for him," Foley said with amusement. He was smiling, affable again. Once more the situation was his to control. He laughed aloud—at her. "This is temporary, Dell. Remember that. Every time you get to feeling this way for a man—it's temporary."

"Except with you, Ed."

"You stray now and then," he said, "but you always come back, don't you? You have to, Dell." He was mocking her now.

"Maybe someday," she retorted.

"Don't let this be that time. Remember: *I don't have to have Marlin alive.*"

She faced him, fighting his contempt and coldness, and then her shoulders slumped wearily. "I'll remember, Ed," she said in a dull voice.

The street door swung open and she straightened. "I'd like that ad placed as soon as possible, Mr. Foley."

"I'll take care of it, Mrs. Ryan. Thank you."

She went on out. A tall, gangling stranger in worn, almost shabby, range clothes held the door for her.

As it swung shut, she heard the man say, "I just drifted in. Figured you might know where a man could get a punching job."

"Offhand, no," Foley said quickly, Dell caught the distaste in his voice.

The door closed behind her and she went on up toward the Mercantile. That, she thought, was the type of reception Rick would have received had he drifted in broke. Almost automatically, he would have been suspect. A man without money was nothing to strangers.

The thought of Rick was strong in her mind, warming her. She glanced back toward the *Clarion* office and shivered a little. She would have to remember Ed's warning.

Rick's trip seemed painfully slow to him. A three-day ride deposited him in Spokane Falls and there be had to wait an indeterminate time before starting back. He could have made the ride faster—one full day over the hills to the railpoint—had he chosen to push the horse faster. But he found it as poor an animal as it looked and he discovered that he was in little better shape himself. In one way, he was glad for the necessary wait. It would give him time to regain his strength.

He had kept off the main trail through the gap, swinging wide along the edge of DR holdings and those belonging to Miles Owen. Halfway between the valley and the railroad, he had hesitated before entering the gap itself when he saw a few brokendown buildings, some showing signs of life. But he went on, pushing the horse as rapidly as possible. He judged the place to be

35

what those tucked into mountain gaps often were—an outlaw hang-out.

At the little town where he caught the train, he turned the horse loose, threw his warbag on the train's one coach and headed south for Spokane Falls.

Here he outfitted himself with Dell's money—clothes, horse, fancy saddle, all the things he would need in his new role. He settled down to impatient waiting until the newspaper appeared with the advertisement he wanted; then he saddled up, and rode to Riverbend.

The river and the town looked placid as he rode down the slope to the ferry. It was a warm, calm day, and the forest on the far side made a sharp contrast to the desert on this shore. Rick studied the land, noting how the timber varied from heavy to scattered and how well-grassed were the great patches of grazing land. It looked like good country, good for cows and good for a man, and he could see why Miles had been attracted to it.

The pleasure left him as he saw the ferry coming from the opposite shore. He tried to rid himself of the feeling that he would be recognized at once, knowing that to succeed in what he had in mind, he would have to bluff colossally. He wanted enough time to size up the situation here. He had no trust in Dell, little belief in what she had told him. But he had played it as she so obviously wanted it played, hoping he could get the reason for this pressure against Miles Owen.

Now he was almost impatient to see the reaction of the ferryman, wondering if this dude-dressed Rick Marlin would be recognizable as the ragged, bearded man who had ridden across in the dark some weeks before.

The ferry docked and a team drawing a loaded wagon

creaked off. Rick rode his horse aboard and dismounted, leaning against the rail and watching the old man work his controls. When they were under way, he said casually, "Have much business?"

John Amos regarded him thoughtfully and then spat into the water. "Some—more at roundup time."

"You don't freight cattle on this thing, do you?"

"Sometimes I freight rattlesnakes," the old man said. Then he cackled. "Hardly, mister. The beef goes through the gap yonder to the rails. But I get them that drifts in and out of here."

Rick was silent now, figuring that the old man had had opportunity enough to hear his voice. They were past midstream when Amos spoke again.

"I been around here longer'n any man and I never forget a face. But I don't recollect yours."

The old man spat again when Rick said, "I'm just up from New Mexico."

"I never forget a voice, either," he observed. He stared into Rick's steady dark gaze. "Nor a favor." The old man scratched his beard with one ancient hand. "For instance, there was a fellow helped me out a few weeks back when I got hurt one night. Him and a little Mexican friend of his. I heard later that this fellow was wanted for murdering Tim Higgins, the deputy marshal here. Didn't act like no murderer to me. I was glad to hear he got plumb away."

"What about his Mexican friend?" Rick asked.

"There's a place in the hills—little town called Kettle Hollow—where I figured he'd be safe from the likes of some in this town. I hear he went there."

The ferry edged to the dock and a rider waiting on the bank started forward. The old man said, "Dollar a head, man and beast," and took Rick's proffered five dollars

37

in gold from his hand.

"Buy yourself a drink," Rick said, and climbed into the saddle.

At the top of the hill, Rick took his first daylight look at Riverbend. It was busy now with people going in and out its half-dozen business houses, with horses and carriages and spring wagons tied along the edge of the boardwalk. Turning his horse over to the hostler in the livery barn, he took his bag and walked the short block to the hotel. There he registered as Richard Carlson, Albuquerque, New Mexico, choosing Albuquerque because he was fairly familiar with the town.

The lobby was half-filled with men and Rick climbed the creaking stairs feeling the speculative eyes of everyone on him. This was the chance he would have to take, he knew, and he was relieved when he closed the door of his room behind him.

Stripping to the waist, he washed the trail dust from himself, then brushed his fawn-colored California trousers and Stetson, wiped the dirt from his boots, and got ready to go back downstairs.

Rick stood in the dining-room doorway, looking down the aisle with its long tables on either side. All of them were filled with men busily eating. Rick saw no one he recognized until a paunchy man near the center stood up and started out. Beside the seat he had occupied, Rick made out the red hair and beard of the man called Ed Foley. He hesitated only briefly and then walked up and seated himself. Foley was bent over his plate and didn't even glance up.

Rick ate slowly, giving Foley a chance to look him over when he finally stopped concentrating on his dinner and leaned back. Rick was down to coffee and pie before Foley acted aware of him. Then he reached over and flicked the top of the newspaper sticking conspicuously from Rick's pocket.

"Just in from the Falls?"

"Yes. Your business?"

Foley took no affront but smiled in a friendly fashion. "My business," he said. "I run the newspaper here. Any visitor is news."

Rick said, "I'm just looking around. There's no news in me."

Foley glanced at their empty coffee cups and signaled the waitress for more. Then he dug into his pocket and brought out a filled pipe and lighted it. When he had the pipe going satisfactorily, he flicked the paper again.

"Mind if I look at it?"

Rick handed him the paper. "Spokane Falls should send you a free copy."

Foley was either thick-skinned or acting deliberately ignorant. "They do, but the mail stage isn't in yet," he said. He unfolded the paper and settled behind it. The coffee came and Rick blew idly on his while he waited. He rolled a cigarette and smoked, nervous inside but not letting any of it appear on the surface. He didn't think Ed Foley had seen him that night of the hunt, and yet he couldn't be sure.

Foley grunted as he read. Suddenly he gave an extra loud grunt and Rick knew that he had found Dell's advertisement. It was plainly ringed with a heavy pencil mark.

Foley returned the paper. "Thanks," he said. "If I can steer you around, call on me. I'm Foley of the *Clarion*."

"Appreciate it," Rick said. He watched idly as Foley threaded his way gracefully between the benches and started down the aisle. He seemed a likable-enough person, Rick thought. He found it hard to connect this man with the bull-voiced leader of the posse. There had been a commanding ruthlessness about him that night, a driving will that had bent the others to him. But today he seemed mild, quite easygoing.

Rick left the table and took the time to smoke a cigar while he strolled through the warm afternoon and looked over the town. So far, he had no plan in mind for seeing Miles and he hoped that the way the town lay might bring him an idea. He wanted to see Miles either with a legitimate excuse at his office, or in absolute secrecy at home.

Miles Owen's office, he found, was the one brick structure in town. It sat on a wide lot, a narrow two-story affair, with Ed Foley's *Clarion* plant directly across the street from it. As Rick passed, he looked up and saw OWEN BUILDING in stone over the doorway and thought how typical that was of Miles. He would have built solidly had this been the only building in Riverbend.

Rick swung around, past the *Clarion* office, by the Mercantile and barber shop, the hotel, crossed the side street, worked past the dressmaker's the hardware, and finally the jail. He did not hesitate as he saw the marshal standing in the sun on the steps talking to a lanky, big-jawed man, The marshal glanced up as Rick drew abreast of him.

"Stranger?"

Rick turned and saw that by daylight the marshal was shorter than he had appeared at night. He was a fattish man, with loose jowls and sweating from his fat. He had the small eyes and loose mouth of a man who tries to be crafty but is more often just venal.

"Stranger," Rick said as if the question were a common one. He went toward the marshal. "Richard

40

Carlson, Albuquerque, New Mexico, Sheriff. Don't tell me I've broken a law."

He was facing the marshal now, letting the man scrutinize him carefully. He waited while the small eyes took in the fifty-dollar Stetson, the expensive boots and pants and vest. As he waited, he saw the growth of a fawning respect.

"No law broke. And it's marshal, not sheriff." He held out a stubby hand. "Name's Hib Bender. Welcome to Riverbend, Mr. Carlson. Staying a while?"

"I hope to go into business here," Rick said easily. He took the hand and then shook with the man standing alongside the marshal. He was introduced as Pryor, who ran the grocery. Rick felt certain he had seen the man in the second posse group, but there was no sign of recognition.

They chatted briefly, then Rick turned, crossed the street and went on down the other side past the bank and the River Bar Saloon. Finally he neared the Owen Building again. He quickened his step to go by rapidly and nearly ran into a girl coming out the doorway.

He threw out an arm and righted her as she slipped in avoiding him. "Sorry. I—" The words choked back in his throat. His arm dropped as if it had been burned. It was Nan Owen.

"Sorry, Miss," Rick said loudly. He tipped his hat and started on, feeling the sweat come out on him, feeling his heart jump.

A man's deep voice came from the building doorway. "You hurt, Nan? You there—wait a minute!"

Rick stopped, and turned. The old familiar command, compelling without arrogance, was in the voice. "I'm sorry," he said. "I don't think she's much shaken up."

He was conscious of the broad glass window of

41

Foley's *Clarion* office directly across the street from where they stood. He and Miles faced each other, Rick a little taller, Miles broader through the body. Rick's equilibrium was completely awry. Seeing Nan with so little warning, then hearing Miles' familiar voice—he had not prepared himself for this.

Miles, he saw, had changed a great deal in five years. Here was no sun-reddened cattleman but a well-dressed businessman wearing fine broadcloth stretched to the bursting over his massive shoulders. In the old days, Miles had let his beard grow during the week and had shaved clean for Saturday night. Now he wore a trimmed goatee and mustache, both threaded lightly with silver. But his eyes were the same—large and dark and penetrating. The mouth was the same too—full but not loose—and, as always, twisted with humor. Miles invariably acted as if he regarded life as a game to be enjoyed.

There was no sign of recognition from either Nan or Miles. "I'm all right," she said. "I'm not hurt, really."

Her voice, Rick noticed, had grown up along with her; it was rounded and mellow rather than shrill and piping. She was slim and blonde, and at first glance showed no resemblance to Miles. But a second look made obvious the similarity around the eyes and in the quirk of the mouth and the movements of the head.

"I apologize again," Rick said, tipping his hat and walking on. He wondered what Nan thought of this small-town life. She had been raised in San Francisco by her mother's well-to-do parents and had visited Miles only during the summer. She had loved the ranch, but an isolated small town in a far corner of the country might be a different thing entirely.

Whenever Rick had thought of her in the past years,

42

he remembered her most often as he had first seen her—a girl of ten learning to ride and rope and shoot under his tutelage. To a fifteen-year-old boy she was a nuisance with her tricks and gabble, and he had often told her so. But she had been a good pupil, learning rapidly the trick of drawing her .38 from its holster and putting out the five hearts in a playing card from twenty feet away. She had learned the trick and then shown it to Miles as a present for his birthday. That had been the year she was fourteen, Rick remembered. He smiled at the way she had complained, wanting to give it up but not being allowed to because she had begged to learn it and he felt the discipline was good for her.

Rick wondered if she still smoked and, if so, did she do as she had in those days—by taking a little tobacco and a little paper now and then from Miles' stock until she had her own makings to carry about.

Rick had learned to his embarrassment that she had done many of the things she had because she admitted that he was her ideal. But now he found it hard to visualize this soft-voiced young woman as the girl who insisted on learning to ride and rope and shoot as well as any man. He thought then of the faint aura of tomboy about her and decided that it must be because she still wore her hair short—a mass of golden ringlets—rather than as the style demanded, long and ornately kept.

His reminiscences were broken off sharply as he heard Ed Foley's voice. "You almost had an accident, friend."

Rick glanced up. "Almost," he said. He started to go on.

"You really looking for a place to settle?" Foley persisted.

"Just looking," Rick said noncommittally. "I told you

43

I wasn't news."

Foley seemed unaware of Rick's shortness. "I saw you stand up to Miles Owen. That's news."

"If you mean the man across the street, he didn't look like trouble."

"He isn't, unless you cross him. The mail stage comes in today and the Spokane Falls paper will be on it."

"So?"

"So maybe somebody else will get interested in buying half of the DR."

"All right," Rick said with dry humor, "I'll go tend to my business so you'll have a story for your next paper."

Laughing, Foley returned to his office. Rick walked on to the livery, asked directions to the DR, and started out. He walked the horse until he was well out of town and then spurred swiftly along the trail he had been forced to leave for the safety of the forest a few weeks ago.

When he rode into the yard, Dell was on her veranda. She was in his arms almost before he took his foot from the stirrup. He felt the demanding warmth of her kiss and he pushed her almost roughly aside.

"You did come back!" she cried. "And anyway, Windy is out on the range."

He led her inside before he gave her the kiss she sought and the assurances she wanted. Finally they sat down to discuss their business. Rick studied her warily. No matter what her action in taking him in and then offering him this chance might mean, there was a different danger to consider. She was a woman who thought she was in love.

"It worked too perfectly," he said. "This Foley fell for my trick. So did the marshal. No one acted as if they had ever seen me."

44

"And you're worried?"

"I'm, always worried when things are too slick. I'll be glad when this business is at in end."

"An end?" Her mouth tightened perceptibly.

"The ugly part of the business," he amended quickly. He crossed to where she sat, smiling down at her.

She was trembling. "I'm afraid," she whispered. "I'm afraid for you."

"So am I," Rick said, but he meant something entirely different.

CHAPTER 5

THE TRANSACTION AT THE BANK, WITH RICK GIVING A small sum to bind the deal, went through—as Rick put it—as smooth as sheep butter. But when Grebs, the banker, directed them to Miles Owen to see about the abstract of title Dell's expression lost some of its pleasure.

Outside the bank, she looked nervously at Rick. "I didn't know this was necessary. Do you . . ."

He shrugged her hand from his arm. "Here comes that newspaperman," he warned.

Foley was angling across the street to greet them both. "So I was right and you're taking in a partner, Dell." His sharp glance traveled slowly over her face. "You don't look exactly pleased."

"There's so much bother," she said quickly. "We have to see Miles. He won't like losing a chance on the property he wanted."

"What can he do?"

Dell still looked displeased, but she smothered it and introduced Rick as Richard Carlson. They shook hands

45

formally. Then Foley said, "Glad to make our meeting official. By the way, I want a story from you on this and I'm willing to pay for it. When your business is done, have dinner with me. Both of you."

"We accept," Dell said. She put her arm through Rick's with a possessive motion that bothered him and they started toward the Owen Building. Foley went on up the street.

"Don't act as if you owned me," Rick said.

She jerked her arm away and stalked ahead, a half-step at first, but by the time they reached the building, she was back, walking demurely at his side.

Rick was wondering what Miles would think. But there was no way around it, and so he escorted Dell up the stairs to a door that had Miles' name in gold leaf on the panel.

There was a reception room filled with heavy red plush furniture, an oak desk, and behind the desk Nan Owen neatly attired in a severe shirtwaist. She nodded without warmth to Dell and looked with no expression at Rick. There was nothing beyond polite inquiry in her blue eyes.

When they stated their business, Nan rose and went into an inner room. In a moment she opened the door and asked them to follow.

Miles was behind a massive desk. He rose as Dell entered, shook hands perfunctorily with Rick as they were introduced, and resumed his seat.

"Carlson? Ever been around San Francisco?"

"This is the farthest west I've been," Rick said. He was thinking that Miles' once work-calloused hands were as smooth as a baby's, and the change bothered him.

Miles was obviously relaxed. He took the information

he needed and then said to Dell, "I didn't realize you were that hard up."

"I want to expand," she said, and left it at that.

When they rose to leave, Miles said to Rick, "I play stud at the River Bar every evening. Drop in for a game now that you're my new neighbor, Carlson."

"I'll do that," Rick said without enthusiasm. He and Dell left, walking by Nan's desk as if it were not there. On the stairs, he said, "You aren't very cordial to the man who has you over a barrel. Sweet talk will get you more than spitting."

"I don't feel like sweet-talking the man who killed my husband."

"You aren't sure of that," he pointed out.

She stopped and faced him. "I have no proof a court would take. But I am sure. So is half of Riverbend. You'll find that out."

"Nevertheless," Rick said quietly, "I'm here to help you. Let me handle it my way—for a while, at least."

Dell studied him, her eyes sharp, and then she looked away. "All right, Rick. If that's what you want—" She broke off and raised her eyes again. His fingers touched her arm. "Whatever you want, Rick . . ."

"Be careful," he warned again.

It had never before occurred to Rick to use a woman. But he saw that he must use Dell—it was his one chance to help Miles and himself. Still, he edged away from the idea, realizing that should her love turn she could be a very dangerous woman.

But he had gone too far—he could not turn away now. He smiled and took her arm and led her to the street.

Miles Owen watched speculatively from his office

window as Dell and Rick finally appeared below and went across the street to the *Clarion* office. A frown brushed across his finely cut features at the way Dell's hand rested so possessively on Rick's arm. And, for that matter, at the dude way Rick was dressed.

"Trying to figure this out, Dad?"

Miles turned to his daughter and the frown erased itself from his forehead. "If we hadn't seen Pancho, I'd be worried. As it is, I don't like what I see. I didn't like it when Windy told me Dell took Rick in and supposedly hid him from Ed Foley. I liked it less when Rick rode out on the quiet without contacting me. Now I see him all duded up and becoming a partner in the DR."

"From the way she acts, she owns Rick *and* the ranch," Nan said.

"Meow," Miles said. But he was smiling. "You haven't changed your feelings about Rick, have you?"

"Dad, I don't believe anything is wrong. Rick is too honest. He's been too close to us."

"Still, if that's Lazy M money he's using to buy into the DR with . . ."

She walked up to him and took his hands. "Don't doubt Rick. He came here to help; we know that."

"How could he know we needed help?" Miles demanded.

"Let's go home to supper," she said quickly. In the doorway, she paused. "He knew because I sent him a telegram," she confessed.

Miles was silent. Then he said, not commenting on her revelation, "It's hard to lose faith in Rick Marlin. But I'll have to wait until I talk to him." He added almost fiercely, "And I'll have to know soon where he stands. They're closing in on us. We haven't got much

48

time left. We haven't got much of anything left."

"We have Rick and Pancho," Nan said stubbornly.

He squeezed her shoulder. "I hope so. I only hope so." And then he said softly to himself, "But are they enough now?"

After dinner, Foley took Rick and Dell to his shop to talk. Squatting on a roll of newsprint, he looked like a great shaggy red bear except for the pipe that jutted from his beard.

He said, "This is different from ranching in New Mexico, Carlson."

"I got a crew," Rick said. "I cull and sell at roundup this fall, saving as many as we have hay to winter-feed, and in the spring we bring in a stronger strain. What's different about it?"

Foley looked at Dell. She was smiling as if she were wholly satisfied with life at the moment, as if she would enjoy being a rancher's wife. "Have you told him, Dell?"

"I'm no fool, Ed. Of course I have."

"She's told me," Rick said. "I've seen this sort of thing before. I still say, what's different about it?"

"Miles Owen," Foley said in a flat voice. He lit the pipe he held. "He's no opportunistic land-grabber pushing the Spanish-Americans off their land. He's a smart man, a big man with money to burn and men to waste. He's Flying M and he's in a position to squeeze DR—and he's doing it. But he's clever. No man in Riverbend can put a finger on any one thing and say—Owen did this. And if they did, he has a crew of hardcases to make them forget what they know."

Rick wanted to say, " You're a liar and you know it. Miles never cheated any man." With an effort, he kept

49

his expression impassive, his eyes on the cigarette he was shaping. "I can get some hardcases myself."

"Is that the way you plan to fight Owen?"

"Can you think of a better way?" Rick demanded. "I figure if you'd done so, things would have been cleaned up long ago. One man can't stand against a united countryside."

Foley was silent and Rick saw that he had touched a weak point in the man's story. When Dell said, "They've needed a leader. They're afraid to move," he had to admire her quick wit.

"Like I told Dell, Foley," he said, "I'll see how far I can sweet-talk this Owen. I've already got an invite to play poker with him. If he doesn't soften up—then I'll do it the hard way."

"Watch him when he deals," Foley said.

Rick said softly, "I've dealt a few hands myself, *amigo*."

Later, after Rick and Foley had escorted Dell home and were riding back, Foley said, "I don't think she liked my coming along, Carlson."

"Meaning what?" Rick let his eyebrows go up.

"You married?"

"No. There isn't even a rope looped for me."

"There might be now. Lots of people here like Dell, Carlson. It wouldn't do a man any good to try to take advantage of her because she's a woman."

Rick was suddenly aware that Foley was jealous of Dell's attitude toward him. He was silent a moment and then he said, "Business is business with me, Foley. I've sunk all I have into this venture. If Dell goes along with the ranch, I suppose I'll take it as part of the bargain. A man could do worse, I imagine."

Foley's silence told Rick that he had puzzled the

newspaperman with his callousness. Still, Rick was worried. A jealous Foley might be even more of a problem than one apparently crusading against Miles Owen. Rick wondered if Foley were jealous of Miles' interest in Dell Ryan, if that might be the reason for his antagonism.

Back at Riverbend, Rick had a brief supper and then crossed the street to the River Bar. It was filled with cowhands, miners, a few with the mark of the woodsman about them, a sprinkling of townspeople, and a handful of rivermen. At this hour of the night the place was quiet and respectable enough. It was, Rick thought, the kind of saloon Miles would like to come to.

He stood in the doorway surveying the scene, wondering if Sid Cutter or any of his crew might be there. At the moment, he saw no one he recognized even vaguely except for Miles sitting alone at the rear. Deliberately he bought a beer and took it to where Miles was shuffling a deck of cards.

"I'm Carlson," he said. "The man you did business with today. Any objections to a friendly game?"

Miles took an expensive cigar from his mouth and shook his head. "I only play stud."

"Like it myself," Rick said loudly. He took a seat and watched Miles' clever fingers riffling, the deck. "Drink?"

"Never use it. I'll take some tea, though."

When the waiter came, Rick asked for a refill on his beer and tea for Miles. He almost said, "Boil it hard," but he swallowed the words back in time.

There was a flicker in Miles' eyes as Rick's mouth opened, closed, and he gulped. Miles said, "You know how I like it, Mike. Boil hell out of her."

Rick flicked a gold eagle on the table as the waiter

51

left.

"That won't buy anything," Miles told him. Rick added another eagle to the first. Miles matched him and they bought chips. Rick looked at the few he held.

He thought, Once Miles dreamed of high stakes. Now he can afford them. And he wondered again if this might not have changed Miles. But looking at the man, he saw beneath the polished surface, and he knew as he had always known that basically Miles was the same.

When the beer and tea came, Miles offered Rick a cigar. He accepted it, noting again the flicker in Miles' eyes. He said, "No, I never could stand a cheap cigar. Some say a man should smoke the best or none at all."

"I'm not fussy. I smoke what I can afford. I figure it's better to do most things that way." Miles dropped the deck. Rick cut and Miles dealt.

Rick wondered if he could count all the nights they had played this game by the low-turned light of their one oil lamp. They had used a greasy deck that had finally become so dog-eared that a man knew by their shape the value of most cards. This was a new deck and Miles handled it no differently. He made a mock scrutiny of the back of each card before dropping it to the table. But Rick had no worries. Miles had shown him how to deal a hot hand, but neither had ever done so in a game.

There was no one close to them, no one paying attention. Rick said in a voice low enough to cut under the hum of talk around the room:

"I was warned about the way you deal."

Miles' lips flickered at the corners. "I'm a first-class bastard," he said, and dropped Rick's second card.

Rick had a four in the hole and a seven showing. Miles displayed a queen and bet white. He handed Rick a five and himself a nine. He bet white again. He dealt Rick a three and himself a queen and doubled his bet, He was just the same, Rick thought, cautious at first but likely to grow reckless as the pace increased.

Miles took time to rap ash from his cigar, gave Rick a six and himself a deuce. He bet blue. Rick raised it a yellow.

"That's ten dollars," Miles said.

Rick nodded. Miles called and showed a deuce in the hole for two pair. Rick said, "Four under for a straight," and reached for the chips. His eyes were on Miles and he saw the man's hand lift as if to stop him. Then Miles settled back and tossed over his cards.

"Shall I show?"

"No need," Miles said in a low voice. There was a faint flush on his cheeks. Rick stacked the chips in silence. Miles had told him more plainly than he needed to that he wasn't sure of Rick—not any longer.

Rick said, "A friendly game."

"Keep it that way."

Rick dealt and lost. Miles won three pots running. Then Rick took a pair and they were back where they had started. A few loiterers came up to watch them but lost interest when the game stayed conservative.

Finally Miles said, "You're a good man to have a game with. How about coming over to my place for a bite to eat? I got a couple of birds the other day and they're roasted to a turn."

Rick saw that no one was taking the suggestion at more than face value, and rose. They cashed their chips and started out together. Miles elbowed ahead, pushing at the crowd that had formed along the bar. Rick followed in his wake, noticing that a few men gave pleasantly enough, but that too many scowled at Miles' back after he passed. Halfway along, a man let out a cry and Rick felt heavy fingers drop on his arm.

"That's him! That's the one that shot Tim Higgins!"

Rick and Miles turned and Rick looked into a face altogether too familiar. He had last seen it above a horse, surprise bulging the eyes as his own forearm drove the man from the saddle to the long, sighing prairie grass.

For a painful moment, Rick was motionless. He had become careless, he realized. The ease with which things had gone since his latest arrival in Riverbend had softened him.

He said quietly, holding his voice down by an effort, "Sorry, *hombre.* You've got the wrong man." He used the tone he would to a drunk.

The man, stocky and unshaven, was obviously sober. He said, "That's him," stubbornly. "That's the one that shot Tim Higgins The one we cornered and who got my rig. That's him!"

Rick stood with his eyes fixed on the man. Slowly his expression became one of bewilderment. He shook his head. "I don't know who Tim Higgins is. I don't know what you're talking about." He glanced toward Miles, who was quiet, waiting. "I'm afraid . . ."

Miles said, "Dud, you're drunk again."

Dud shook his head, a stubborn look settling on him. "I ain't drunk, damn it! This is the one . . ."

Ed Foley came down from the far end of the bar. In the press of men, Rick had not seen him before. Now, Foley said, "Dud, you're loco. Carlson here just rode in from Spokane Falls a few days ago." Dud's face grew red. Foley went on, "Besides, you said he had a beard. You're just imagining—"

"Put a beard on him and see!" Dud half-screamed.

Foley laughed, and others, taking the cue, followed suit.

Dud clamped his lips shut and swung to the bar. "To hell with it," he growled. "Gimme a drink."

"Who was that man?" Rick inquired as he and Miles started down the boardwalk.

"A range hand," Miles answered. "He's a good worker when he isn't loaded."

"I wonder who I'm supposed to look like," Rick said, and dropped the subject.

They crossed the street and Miles led the way through the alley to his imposing house. "Why," he said in answer to Rick's question, "like the man who shot Tim Higgins, the deputy marshal, and laid out the marshal himself with a gun butt. They spotted this fellow trying to crawl into my house through a window. More than a month ago."

"Hardcase, ain't I," Rick observed dryly.

Miles led the way up the veranda, opened the door, and ushered Rick in. Once the door was closed, he said, "Nan's asleep, Rick. We'll go into the kitchen."

There, he stirred the stove and built up the fire to make coffee. He set a roast pheasant on the table, laid out bread, butter and cream, and when the coffee was done settled down to eat, his collar open and his shoes off. Rick ate in silence, thinking how Miles had always hated tight things on himself, especially the feel of a tight rein.

When they were done, Miles reached for a cigar and Rick took out his tobacco. Miles said, "Were you trying to get in here, Rick?"

Rick paused in rolling his cigarette and lifted his eyes to Miles' face. The dark eyes were fixed on Rick questioningly. He wondered how to handle this now. Before, he knew, he would have told it straight out. But

55

since he had heard so many things, since he had tied in with Dell . . .

Miles broke into his thoughts. "One of the boys at my ranch found a saddled cayuse a few weeks ago. There were soogans behind the saddle. They had some things rolled up in them. The stuff is out at my ranch now."

Rick lowered his head and finished rolling his cigarette. "No," he said, "I wasn't trying to break in. I spotted this as your house. I saw this man you say is the marshal trying to pry your window open. I jumped him. I figured you might have got big enough to have enemies, Miles. His deputy drew on me and I went for his gun. It went off while we were fighting—that's all."

"And the posse went after you?"

"Yes." Rick paused and added, "So quick that they must have been saddled and waiting to ride."

"But you lost your horse and still got away?"

"I jumped friend Dud and got his outfit."

"And came back looking like this?" Rick only shrugged. Miles said, "It's your business. But you came to me in the dark—wshy?

This, Miles had a right to know. Rick said slowly, "To bring you a message, Miles. From myself."

"All the way from Arizona—one you couldn't write?"

"One I couldn't write," Rick agreed. "I got run off the place down there. If I could have written it, there was no place for you to send an answer. Anyway, I had no chance to get to Tucson."

Miles nodded, showing his awareness that Rick was still trying to keep Miles Parker of Arizona from being connected with Miles Owen of Riverbend, Washington Territory.

"You need help? A crew?"

56

"There isn't anything left for a crew to work," Rick answered. "Besides, I'm wanted there—for murder. So is Pancho." He saw Miles' startled look. "Pancho came with me. I thought he might have seen you by now."

Miles shook his head. "I've been away—I was away the night you were 'protecting' me. No, I haven't seen Pancho." Abruptly, he sat up straight. "This doesn't tie, Rick. You and Pancho aren't killers."

"Neither are you," Rick said dryly, "but you're wanted there."

Miles waved a neat hand. "That was an old-time feud. I just didn't play it smart. Now I know better. Anyway, I think I can clear that charge whenever I want to. But you . . ."

"I killed a man," Rick admitted. "They charged Pancho with collusion."

"Self-defense?"

"Defense of the ranch—I claim."

"Against who, for God's sake?" Miles demanded.

"A bunch of roughs I never saw. They appeared about a year ago and started picking off our beef and cutting our fence. When we finally figured out what was going on, we roughed back. Then they burned us out." He stopped and the bitterness came back strongly. "Manuel and Josefa didn't get away. This crew just let them burn."

"And all this time you never saw them?"

"Not their faces," Rick said. "They were masked. They layed it careful. I did see one." he amended. "He got too close once and I climbed him. He got away but lost his bandanna. I saw him again a few days later in town. I drew and shot him."

"And Pancho?"

"Pancho carved our brand on him. A big howl went

57

up from the drifters in town and someone started pushing for a lynching. I didn't stop to be charged. Coming through Oregon, Pancho and I saw a dodger that was out for us."

Miles sucked on the stub of his cigar. "About a year ago," he murmured. "Burned out. The beef all gone."

"They cleaned us," Rick said. "And then we were trailed here."

Miles didn't seem surprised. "What do you plan to do?"

Rick spread his hands. "You're the boss. I'm only ramrodding the outfit."

Miles stirred. "I wanted the money from this year's sales, I need it badly."

Rick shook his head. "There were no sales—there was no beef to sell. I'm flat, too, Miles. Oh, there's money in Tucson, but I don't dare go for it now."

"No," Miles agreed. He raised his heavy eyebrows. "But you managed to buy a piece of the DR."

Rick made a slow move toward his coffee "cup. This was the part he hadn't wanted to get into just yet.

"Why do you want the DR, Miles?"

"Let me ask a question first," Miles said. He took a last draw on his cigar, wrinkled his nose at the bitterness of the butt, and lighted a fresh one. "What have you heard about me?"

Rick said frankly, "If I'm working against you, Miles, I can't say."

"I don't know where you stand, Rick. But you don't know anything I haven't heard before. If you have and start saying something, I'll chop you off."

Rick knew that he would. He didn't doubt Miles' sense of fairness. "I've just heard you're after the DR and Dell Ryan both. That you've been after them one

58

way and another for better than a year."

"One way and another," Miles murmured. "Such as rustling beef, cutting fence, bogging cattle, burning hay, and—killing husbands." He lifted his eyes to Rick. "Does that sound like me?"

"Damn it, Miles, no! But you wanted to know what I've heard, and that's it."

"I'm the big bad ogre here," Miles said. "I came five years ago when this wasn't even a good hole in the ground. There were two stores, one of them a saloon. I homesteaded a likely looking piece back of one of the few ranches—that's now the DR. When I tried to expand I found out why the land hadn't been taken up before. I jumped too fast, as usual."

"Not enough water?"

"Not certain water," Miles said. "And I lie wrong to run much beef. My hay land is short, too. The home place is big enough to squeeze out a living and that's about all."

"How did you expand, Miles?"

Miles had to smile. "I bought, Rick. I bought openly and fairly. I started this town going and I set up a real estate business to take advantage of it. I sold things cheap to get people to come here. I overstocked my own place to encourage others to come. I built this town. For a while they flooded in here. But now that they're settled and solid, I'm the big bad ogre who's trying to rob widows!"

"Why didn't you buy the DR?"

"Dell's husband inherited it," Miles explained. "I tried to buy from the old duffer that had it but he wouldn't sell. 'Leaving it to my grandnephew,' " Miles mocked. "And so he did." He rapped ash from his cigar and regarded Rick with a faint smile. "I wanted it as

59

badly after I'd been here a year as I want it now. Worse, maybe, because I was just getting started and didn't have much to bargain with. Does that mean anything to you?"

"I'm supposed to ask why you didn't go after the old man. Why you waited until Dell and her husband, got it before trying the rough way."

"Yes," Miles agreed. "Why didn't I? The old man would have been easier. There wasn't any law here to stop me, then. Why didn't I?"

"Because you don't operate that way, Miles." Rick finished his coffee and rose. "Miles, I don't like to be playing the other side. But I'm into this—I'm in across the fence."

"I know," Miles said. His smile was calm. "Rick, what if someone told you I'd been losing beef, too. That I've had fences cut and hay burned—what then?"

"You're doing it to make things look good for yourself," Rick said. "You can stand it better than she can. Is that the answer?"

"It's the one I get," Miles said. He got up to see Rick to the door. "The town believes what it wants to believe, not what makes sense. It came slowly, that belief—as if someone was putting poison into people's minds a drop at a time."

Miles opened the front door. "Play the hand any way you like, Rick. Think what you like. But no matter how you figure it, drop in for poker sometimes. Any time."

"I'll do that, Miles," Rick said. He walked on out and heard the door close softly behind him.

Miles was letting him make up his own mind. And when he had done so, Miles would expect him to come and state his position. If Rick wanted to believe that

60

Miles was running roughshod over a defenseless woman, then Miles wasn't going to make any effort to change Rick's opinion. If Rick chose to come around to Miles' point of view, if he could honestly accept what Miles had hinted at—that he was the injured party—then Miles would accept that and be glad for the help Rick could give him. Meanwhile, it was up to Rick to make his own decision.

Walking carefully, Rick felt his way across the dark yard toward the carriage house. He had almost reached it when quick footsteps from behind brought him to a halt. Stepping swiftly into a puddle of shadow, he drew his gun and turned. He peered through the heavy blackness in the direction from which he had come.

A white face loomed up; a stray bit of light from a distant house picked at golden hair. It was Nan.

"Rick!"

Somehow she was in his arms and she was crying. Rick held her, patting her head as awkwardly as he had the time she had fallen from a mean bronc and skinned herself thoroughly. Only now he felt even more awkward. Here was no gawky kid in cut-down man's jeans but a warm, vibrant young woman. The faint scent of her perfume rose to his nostrils and he was acutely aware that she wore only a light wrapper over an equally light nightgown. Gently, he removed her arms from about him and drew her deeper into the shadow.

"This is foolish, Nan. If anyone should see . . ."

She laughed a little, shakily, and wiped away her tears with a quick, characteristic gesture. Reaching into his pocket, she got his handkerchief and blew her nose daintily. She was the old Nan for the moment, the very young Nan.

"I'm sorry, Rick. I didn't think," she said. "I've been

61

so worried and upset that—"

"About Miles? About me?"

"Both," she admitted. "I overheard you." She sounded a little defiant. "I suppose I was—spying, but I can't let Dad go on as he has been and not try to help. Something is bothering him terribly. I know part of it— most of it, I suppose. But there are things he won't tell me."

"He's trying to keep you out of it," Rick guessed. "Well, if you heard us, now you know."

"What do I know? That he's wanted in Arizona on an old murder charge. That you are, too. That the Lazy M is burned out. And," she went on in a flat voice, "that people here think he's riding down Dell Ryan. That isn't true! Ever since I first heard the rumor, I've watched Dad, He's never even had a thought, like that!"

"It's hard to believe of Miles," Rick admitted.

She put a hand on his arm and there was strength in the grip of her fingers. "You can't believe it, Rick. How could you? Don't you know Dad well enough?"

"Men change," Rick said.

"That's what Dad wondered about you," she retorted. "But I don't believe it—not of either of you. Men don't change that much." She took a deep breath and then burst out, "She's made you think that!"

"I do my own thinking," Rick said. "She's told me her side. Miles has told me part of his. The decision is mine. She can't influence me." He took her hand from his arm and held the slender fingers for a moment. And now he found it difficult to think. Dropping her hand, he moved away slightly, irritated at himself. "You came to ask me to help Miles? Is that it, Nan?"

She answered with a question of her own. "Why did you come, Rick?"

62

"To get Miles to help," he answered. "When we were burned out, I knew of only one place to go. I want to find the men that cleaned us out and get back what we've lost. But it's Miles' place—I couldn't do it without him." He paused, aware suddenly that his own thinking needed clarification.

"I don't mean that," she said sharply. "I understand that part. I mean—why did you come back like you are now, on her side of the fence?"

"There was no other way for me to stay in Riverbend," he said. "Dell took me in, saved my life, hid me from Ed Foley and his posse."

"For a purpose!" she murmured savagely. "Rick, be careful of her. She's— Oh, there's something wrong. I've tried and tried but I can't like her."

"Jealous, perhaps?" he said lightly, and then regretted it.

"I suppose I am," Nan admitted heatedly. "But there's more to it than that. I just don't trust her."

"But I can trust Miles?"

"Has he ever failed in a trust?" she demanded bluntly.

"No," Rick said, "he never has—not with me."

"And he hasn't changed," she said hotly. "Do you think a little money, a little success—" She broke off with a short, bitter laugh. "Money, success!" She looked up into Rick's face. "Do you think those might be the things that have changed him?"

"They've changed other men."

"Not Miles Owen," she said. "Because he hasn't got them, He wants them like he wanted them in Arizona— for me. But he won't try to get them any differently than he tried there."

Rick thought of Miles' old code: "Someday I'll be big but I'll be big clean."

Now, Rick said only, "I'm keeping my eyes open, Nan. I'm not swallowing everything that's handed me. But Dell did save my life and I owe her a chance. I have to make my own decision."

"That's all I ask," she said. "Because you're like Dad—you won't have changed, either." With a suddenness characteristic of the old Nan, she flung her arms about his neck and kissed him. For a brief instant her lips were warm on his. Then, turning, she lifted her long wrapper and fled back to the house.

Rick stood watching her until she was out of sight, feeling the warmth of her lips against his mouth and knowing that from now on things could never be the same between himself and Nan.

With one hand reaching for the doorlatch of his room, he stopped. As weary as he was, the light noise from the other side of the door registered on him, drawing back his hand. It had been that way for a long while now. Once you live close to danger, he thought, you are always on the defensive, always wary.

He shook his head to clear it of sleep. Then, with a sudden, darting motion, he turned the latch, thrust the door away from himself, and stepped through the opening. As quickly as he had entered, he flattened himself against the wall to one side of the doorway and slammed the door shut with his hand.

Gun out, he crouched tensely, waiting. There seemed to be nothing but darkness and shadow. The window blind was drawn and no light seeped in around it. The bed made a dark splotch, as did the chair and the dresser. Rick held his breath, and in a moment caught the rough sound of another person's breathing.

He dropped to his knees and eased himself forward, his gun held ready, every nerve alert. He was waiting for the other to break, to act in some way.

The break came when Rick was within three feet of the bed and almost down to the far end. A foot scraped and a form hurtled darkly through the air. Rick straightened and jumped sideways. Someone landed, heels gouging, not inches from where he had been. He lashed out with his gun barrel and heard a grunt of pain. He swung again but caught empty air. As he spun, seeking his assailant, the door was flung open and whoever had been in the room was gone, boots pounding on the bare flooring of the dark hallway.

Rick reached the hall a moment too late. Following at a run, he saw a leg flick out of sight at the foot of the stairs. He raced on down to the lobby, to the front door, and heard the door in the rear slam. Stepping to the street, he waited, looking up toward the crossroads. But no one appeared except Ed Foley in the saloon doorway across the street. Foley stood there a moment as if savoring the fresh air, then he started forward, stopped, and squinted toward Rick. After a minute, he crossed over.

"Having trouble, Carlson?"

Rick glanced down and saw that he still held his gun. He also saw a darkish stain on it. "Prowler," he said, "I got him a lick with my gun sight."

"Anything taken?"

Rick thrust the gun back in his holster and shrugged. "I haven't looked. But there isn't much to take unless he wanted clothes."

"Money?" Foley suggested.

"It's on me or in the bank at home," Rick said.

"Papers?"

"Why would anyone want papers of mine? There aren't any, by the way." He half-nodded to himself as an idea came to him, "Even if I haven't anything to lose, this upset me. I think I'll have a drink. join me?"

Foley shook his head. "I'm off to bed, I've got a job in the morning." He flipped his pipestem at Rick. "*Adios.*"

"*A usted,*" Rick said automatically. Foley looked blank and Rick realized he had spoken in Spanish. He said, still in the same language, "I wonder how many sins that red beard is hiding?" Foley grinned again, looking genuinely uncomprehending, and Rick watched him walk off. For what it was worth, he thought, Foley apparently did not understand Spanish.

CHAPTER 6

FOR A WHILE, RICK DIVIDED HIS TIME BETWEEN THE DR, ostensibly getting things ready for a "change in policy," and town, where he spent a good deal of time in the saloon. He appeared to be playing a lot of poker to kill the time. Actually, he was waiting for developments.

Finally he decided that it was time to move. He had killed too much of the lazy, hazy summer as it was. The sun burned hotly, despite the haze, browning the graze and making a noticeable difference in the water level of the river. But soon it would begin to sharpen a little at night and fall would be a promise and roundup time would be at hand.

Rick's first act was to get a crew for the DR. So far, there was still only Windy. And he seemed to have matters well in hand. For the time, at least, nothing was happening that Miles could be blamed for. When Rick put it up to Ed Foley, he got a concise and logical

66

answer:

"Everyone pools at roundup to drive the beef through the gap to the rails," Foley explained. "Miles won't ask for trouble again until after roundup. Besides, his men have enough work of their own to keep them busy in the summer. It's in the winter that they find other things to occupy them."

Rick made no comment, though he kept Foley's words in mind when he started putting a crew together. At first, he thought of asking help from Miles but decided against it. Despite the fact that he and Miles played a good deal of poker together, there was a mutual agreement between them not to appear too friendly. As a matter of fact, they were not friendly. In a way, there was an armed truce between them, and Rick knew it would continue until he could make up his mind as to the final line he must take.

Rick turned again to Ed Foley. He couldn't help liking the exuberant newspaperman and, as well, he knew that no one was in better touch with the town and country people or with the drifters that came and went through Riverbend.

Foley got to the point immediately. "How much of a crew do you want?"

"Three men should be enough," Rick said. "I have one—so I need two. Windy can boss, I suppose."

Foley sucked on his pipe and leaned back in his swivel chair. Rick knew the question that would come next. "Have you changed your opinion? Do you want to run beef or fight Miles Owen?"

"I want to run beef," Rick said dryly. "If that means fighting Owen, as everyone around here seems to think, then I'll have to fight him."

Foley stopped sucking on the pipe and decided to put

some tobacco in it. "So you haven't changed your mind."

Rick said irritably, "Aren't there men in these parts that can work and fight both?"

Foley's grin was faint. "All the fighting men have seen a cow. I'm not sure how well they could work one."

"I need two men. I'll have to take what I can get."

Foley jammed his pipe back between his teeth and felt around in his coat pockets for a match. When he had one located, he scratched it on his boot sole and lighted his tobacco. He exhaled leisurely. " I'll send you two that know how to work."

"And won't run at the first cut fence?"

"That I can't guarantee."

Rick could only shrug. "Send them out tomorrow so I can take a look at them." He got up, stood a moment while he rolled and lighted a cigarette. When he looked down at Ed Foley, his eyes were a little bleak. "Maybe I'm getting into something I didn't figure on."

"Maybe," Foley agreed. He took the pipe from his mouth and studied the end. "Want to quit? Your draft to New Mexico hasn't cleared yet."

"As good as," Rick said negligently. He let smoke dribble up from his lips, obscuring his face. He had an uneasy feeling that there was more behind Foley's apparently casual remark than appeared on the surface. But what it could be, he wasn't sure. Unless Foley didn't trust him fully. After all, he reminded himself, Foley was a friend of Dell's. He wouldn't want to see her taken in by a stranger.

Rick left, wondering what kind of men Foley would send him.

The next morning, shortly after Rick arrived at the DR, two riders came at an easy pace into the yard and got out of their saddles. Rick was working with Windy, fixing corral posts, and he came across the yard. Dell appeared on the veranda of the small house and looked quizzically at Rick. He called as he walked, "Foley send you?"

"Just this morning," one said. He moved a little toward Rick. The other followed suit. The first man was a tall beanpole Rick had never seen. He was neither young nor old. There were crow's-feet around his eyes from squinting into the sun and his clothes were as patched as his saddle. All of this Rick took in with a practiced glance, along with the fact that, despite the patching, the tall man was neat.

When the other man came into close range, Rick almost broke his stride. He saw the heavy face and the popping eyes of the man called Dud. He became acutely conscious that he was in dirty jeans and needed a shave. For the moment, anyway, he knew that he looked a lot like the man who had knocked Dud off his horse two months back.

Dud grinned, showing one missing front tooth and the other broken. "I see you ain't the man I thought you was, Mr. Carlson. Dirtied, you look less like him than you did slicked up."

That, Rick knew, was a lie. He only said, "I'd about forgotten. You're the one that thought I killed Tim Higgins."

"A mistake," Dud said hastily. He cleared his throat and looked past Rick. "A little too much red-eye, maybe."

Rick introduced them to Dell, finding in the process that the beanpole was named Arkwright Smith and that

69

Dud's last name was Curl. They drifted off to look over the place—bunkhouse, corrals, horse stock, and other things with which they would have to deal. Rick stayed behind to speak with Dell.

"What did Foley mean by sending Dud here?" he asked.

"Maybe to prove that you aren't the man Dud thought you were," Dell suggested. She glanced toward the men walking off, a thin line of worry creasing her forehead. "Still," she said, "I've seen Dud work. He isn't bad unless he's been drinking."

Rick left the decision to Dell. "Hire them?"

Dell continued to look thoughtful. Then she said, "We may as well. Ed knows the men in these parts. Maybe these . . ."

Rick nodded. "Maybe these are the kind I wanted—half-cow nurse and half-fighter."

They left it at that and Rick went off to make the standard offer of thirty a month and found to the men. They accepted and he showed them a few of the things they would be expected to do. Then they took their soogans into the bunkhouse. Since he had already spread his blankets on the bunk nearest the door and Windy had appropriated the one behind it, they tossed their rolls near the back.

"Dinner at twelve," Rick said, as he left. "Windy will square you away."

It was a day later that Pancho drifted in. He came on a well-traveled pony up the Riverbend road, and when he stopped at the ranch house he went to Dell first. He talked to her in a burst of Spanish and then in very bad English. All he seemed to be able to say in English was: "*El Señor* Carlson from New Mexico." Dell finally

70

called Rick over from his work.

Pancho was wooden-faced at Rick's stare. Rick had no more recognition on his own face. He said, "Looking for a job? I'm full."

Pancho only shrugged. He spoke in Spanish, slowly, as if Rick might not understand too well. Rick listened and glanced sideways at Dell. She did not seem to understand. He said to Pancho in slow, clear Spanish, "The lady is beautiful, no? Much fire in the eyes, no?" Dell showed no more expression than before. Rick tried a little vulgarity; still no expression. Satisfied, he let Pancho go on, then he translated for Dell.

"He says his name is Jesus Maria Luis Pedro Zapillo but that he is called Pancho. He is from El Paso, Texas, a fine *vaquero*—cowboy. He is a great fighter and he wants a job. He drifted into town yesterday and heard that we were hiring and that a *Señor* Carlson from New Mexico was here. He hoped I would speak Spanish because he knows very little English. He will work for almost nothing just so he can hear me speak Spanish. He is very hungry because he hasn't been able to get much to eat. He will be my devoted friend; he will be your devoted friend." Rick grinned a little. "For us, he will do anything if we give him a horse and a cow to work, a little food and speak Spanish to him."

Dell laughed, but it was a faint sound. "We already have our crew."

"Still," Rick said slowly, "if he can fight . . ." He asked it of Pancho in Spanish.

"*Si, señor,*" Pancho answered eagerly, turned and squinted up at a tree filled with green apples. His knife appeared with startling suddenness, and a slight whishing sound, and an apple hanging near the top parted from its stem and came tumbling toward the

71

ground. Pancho retrieved it before it struck, picked up his knife which disappeared somewhere about his person, and brought the apple to Dell, presenting it with a graceful bow.

"For the lovely lady," he said. "A gift from my soul."

Rick translated. Dell accepted the apple with a smile of thanks. She was not laughing at Pancho. Her eyes were puzzled but the look on her face was one of pleasure. Rick wondered if she were really gulled. Yet he knew sweet talk had its advantages with Dell.

Pancho spoke again. Rick said, "He can cook, too."

Dell had to laugh. "He's hired, as of now."

Showing Pancho the bunkhouse, where he dropped his miserable roll on the farthest bed, Rick led him to the kitchen. Pancho checked the fire and the wood box, poked in the cupboards, nodded in satisfaction, and waved Rick away.

"I don't think I like this, Rick," Dell said, looking up at Rick when he returned to the living room.

"Pancho? He seems harmless enough," Rick answered.

"Still, it's known you're from New Mexico. El Paso isn't far from there. It might be a way of getting someone here that knew you or of you. Someone that could cause trouble."

"You mean Miles Owen?"

She nodded again. Rick shrugged. "I think Pancho took a chance that a man from New Mexico could speak Spanish. Still, if you'd rather he'd go . . ."

Dell was obviously remembering the speech Pancho had made and the way the knife had cut the stem of the apple. "He might be of value." Her laugh bubbled unexpectedly. "I'll have to learn Spanish, won't I?"

Perhaps she wouldn't have laughed had she seen the

72

two forms which drifted that night from the bunkhouse after the other men were asleep. They stood by the corral and spoke softly in rapid Spanish. It was an asset, Rick realized, that might well pay off.

"Where in hell have you been?"

"I did not need to come into the town," Pancho explained. "The next morning I hid by the ferryman's house. He comes home with his head in a bandage. There is a man with him, helping him. I hear all about how you kill a deputy marshal. I hear that Miles is a bad man, perhaps, but the marshal is a worse one. I hear how some masked men rode down the ferryman and as far as he is concerned they were the sheriff's men. You were good. You got help to him when he was hurt."

Pancho's teeth showed even in the darkness. "I learned a lot from the old man; he hears much on his ferry."

"You stayed there all this time?"

"No," Pancho said. "I spent some of the time in the hills of Miles' ranch. And some time in a place they call the gap."

"I went through it on my way out the first time," Rick remembered. "A broken-down hotel and saloon?"

"*Si*," Pancho agreed. "If you are ever in trouble, that is the place." His smile flashed in the darkness. "There are a few miners, but mostly they are men who play the part of miners, They find it quiet there."

"Without the law bothering them?" Rick suggested.

"*Si*," Pancho said again. "The bartender is a friend of mine. His name is Paco—he liked it better than plain Frank. And there is a miner who has no mine, only a hole in the ground. Him I call Barba Negra. And a fine black beard he had. Remember these things, Rick. If we have to run again—"

Rick broke Pancho's talk off with a quick move of his hand on the other's arm. His ears had caught a rustling sound from behind them. It was not repeated, and after a moment he said, "Tell me the rest tomorrow. We can't stay out too long at a time."

The man who stood not ten feet from them, also in shadow, puzzled trying to catch the sense of what he heard. That failing, he tried to make something by tone of voice but the musical cadences of the language mocked him. He could only tell that it was not anger. He swore to himself. When he reported, he would have to make up some kind of story.

Then he caught the word "Miles." He slipped back to the bunkhouse, his coat rustling lightly against the side of the barn as he moved. He did not hear it; he was too busy concocting a story to hang around the word "Miles," said so easily and familiarly.

In the week that followed, Rick worked with his crew and found them good. Even Dud proved himself to be an adequate man with a cow pony and rope. It was getting toward roundup time and they went over the entire spread, spotting bunches of grazing stock. At the same time, the summer had been a prolonged dry one and so they checked every spring and creek, cleaning them to make sure that adequate water was flowing for the stock to drink.

In that way Rick managed to make himself familiar not only with the workings of the ranch, but with the terrain as well. He would put the men to work cleaning out a spring or making a settling place in a slow-running creek and then ride off to get the lay of the land for himself. He discovered that the DR hay meadow down near the river was of no value this year. An early June cutting had been made and that was all for this season. A fire had "broken out," Dell told him, that had burned the rest of it.

Rick calculated the winter hay and flatly told Dell how many head she could hold over. The biggest proportion she would have to ship out. She acquiesced without appearing to care.

From the occasional comments Dell dropped during their evenings in her parlor, he discovered the reason. Actually, she was not interested in the ranch. She was a city woman in temperament. He made the remark one night, surprised as it was so opposed to her actions and determination when he had first met her.

Dell laughed it off. "Maybe I've just come to trust you, Rick. You take over very well. And I would like to get off the place once in a while. See a new face, buy a new dress, that sort of thing."

The subject was dropped, but Rick noticed that Dell was careful to express more interest in what they did during the days that followed.

Rick spent as much time as he could on the range. Dell was almost too demanding of his time. It was, he thought, as if she owned him.

And after he ran into Nan on the range, he found his stays at the ranch house even less pleasant. He was riding alone along the eastern edge of DR graze, on unfenced land, when he saw a rider in the distance coming from the direction of the Flying M. He stayed where he was until the rider came close enough for him to identify Nan. She rode the same as always, fast but not hard on her horse, sitting the saddle like a burr, her hat caught to her throat by the chin thong and her short golden curls whipped by the breeze her own speed created.

She lifted herself in the stirrups as she neared and gave a war whoop that brought the old days crowding back close to him. He answered and hurried to meet her She drew rein beside him, laughing. The wind had brought color into her cheeks and the sun had sprinkled freckles on her absurdly short nose. Rick had a sudden desire either to pull her off the little sorrel she rode and kiss her or to ride away fast before he did something completely foolish.

"Spying on the Flying M, Rick?"

"I thought you were on the DR," he retorted.

Nan's laugh was gleeful. "This is no-man's land, actually. An old man by the name of Amos who runs the ferry owns it. He won't sell and he won't rent. He insists that it's for the use of everyone. So we both use it."

"Fair enough," Rick agreed. "What brings you out of the office?"

She made a face. "The office! Shirtwaists and skirts," With a twinkle, she took out her sack of tobacco and rolled a cigarette. Rick made a mock scowl as he struck and held a match for her.

Blowing a thin stream of smoke, she said, "Every once in a while I get Dad to break loose and come out for a while. He almost has to when it nears roundup, of course, since it's a job that takes everyone." Her light mood dropped. "Then, this year being so dry, we have more worry than usual over water. We're about frantic trying to move the cattle toward the hills where the creeks and springs are still flowing a little. Even then there isn't enough, really."

"I've noticed that the DR is pretty dry," Rick said. "But if Miles needs water, we have some to spare. Why not turn the beef on the west side up into those hill pockets we have? There's feed and water enough. We can sort out at roundup—"

Nan looked at him in astonishment. "Do you think Dell would permit that?"

"Who'll ask her? I'm running the spread, Nan—for a while, anyway."

She shook her head. "Poor, innocent Rick! What do you think the talk would be when Flying M beef was found at DR water holes?"

Rick said impatiently, "Why take the feud out on cows? Tell Miles that I'll drop a piece of fence and he can run what beef he wants over there. I'll keep my man away. Before roundup, you can have them run back. And if people do find out, I'll give my reasons."

"You're taking a chance," Nan warned him. "It might tie you in to Miles—it might start people asking questions."

"Let it. The whole thing will be over by roundup, anyway. One way or another, this can't go on forever."

"You have a plan?" she asked eagerly.

"Right now, nothing but getting Miles' beef in decent shape to make the drive to the railpoint."

"Dad's beef?"

"And ours," he said, "and anyone else's that hasn't got water."

They parted shortly after that, but in the succeeding days somehow they managed to meet each other quite often. Rick rode with Nan as she worked the Flying M, checking water holes and fence and spotting steers that had drifted into canyons. He learned a good deal about Flying M terrain, too, and he saw that most of Miles' prosperity was on the surface. As things stood, he had a poor grade of stock to work with and only patchy grazing to put them on. Much of his land was timbered or rocky slope with only an occasional grassy draw working back in. His flat graze was often too dry unless he could somehow get water to it, and his hay meadow was hardly adequate for half his stock.

The DR, on the other hand, was almost too swampy in spots, and it lacked timber where there should have been timber. He could understand how the two combined would make a truly fine spread.

On his last trip to see Nan, Rick took Pancho along with him. Pancho hadn't seen Nan since she was a tow-headed kid of fifteen and he looked forward to the meeting. Rick had found it quite a chore to pry Pancho away from Dell, who seemed to admire his kitchen talents greatly, but by using the excuse that Pancho would have to become familiar with the range in order to be an advantage at roundup, he managed.

Now Pancho and Nan were chatting in Spanish, though Nan's was somewhat halting and, as always, sketchy. She listened while Pancho told of his experiences since he and Rick had parted on the riverbank earlier in the summer.

"I've always heard wild stories of the gap," she commented. "But your friends sound like nice people, Pancho."

"*Si*," he answered. "They would cut your throat for a peso. But if you are a friend, they would cut your enemy's throat for nothing."

"I know people who aren't hiding out that do better than that," Nan observed dryly. "They'll cut a friend's throat for nothing."

Rick told her of the "burned out" hay meadow on DR graze. "Miles Owen is responsible, of course," she said.

"No names were mentioned," Rick said. "But the insinuation was there."

78

Nan said quietly, "Well over a year ago, Dad and I were doing fine. Dad practically started Riverbend and a lot of the people who moved in had borrowed from him to get started. And a lot of them haven't paid him back. Naturally they like it when they can find something wrong with him. Maybe they won't have to pay him back if they can drive him out. I think that's the way some figure it."

"Well over a year ago," Rick repeated. "And then what happened?"

"And then," Nan said, "things started happening. The DR began to have trouble—and we were blamed. When we had trouble, it was faked, of course. Then Dell Ryan's husband was killed while riding fence. Dry-gulched. Can you imagine Dad ordering that, Rick?"

Pancho answered for both of them, swearing fervently in Spanish words that Rick hoped Nan was not familiar with. She went on, "Then things let up for a while here. Dad tried to make peace with Dell and she—well, she threw herself at his head, actually. That's when he got the idea that if she wouldn't sell, he might marry her and get the land. You know how Dad will jump at an idea sometimes.

"Look at the Flying M. Right now Owen and Company is all front. Dad lent a lot and sunk what was left into this. He's been trying to get water where it's needed, and he's been hoping to improve his beef strain. He has, actually, about enough cash to buy the DR and that's all. He's really been hurt a lot more than the DR. He's lost more cattle, spent more money repairing fence and cleaning out water holes—everything. He's about strapped."

Pancho swore again. "I heard much of this at the gap," he admitted.

79

Rick wasn't listening. He said thoughtfully, "When things quieted down here—when was that?"

"After fall roundup last year," Nan said promptly "Why?"

"Because," Rick said, "that was about the time they started bothering us down there."

Nan grasped his arm. "Rick—is there a connection?"

Rick said dryly, "I wasn't followed all the way to Riverbend by men that just wanted to see the country."

"Not long before you arrived, Dell changed completely toward Dad. She—oh, I don't know, but I can't help thinking that she's like a puppet. Someone pulls a string and she does one thing; they pull a different string and she does something else."

Rick didn't say anything. When it was time to leave, he rode slowly away with Pancho. They hadn't had time to do much talking and he wanted to find out what else the alert little Mexican had picked up during the time he was hiding out.

"I learned much, Rick," Pancho said. "This man Foley used to call on the *Señora* Ryan often late at night. It is interesting, no?"

"Yes," Rick agreed.

"And one time after you came to town all dressed fine, there was a meeting at a line shack on the Flying M." Pancho smiled reminiscently. "I attended—at the window." He went on, describing how three men had ridden from town and one up from the Flying M. He hadn't seen their faces but the voices he would remember. One was that of Dud Curl, another a broken-nosed man who had been one of Miles' six hands and who, shortly afterward, had been discharged. Pancho had had a letter delivered by one of his "friends" from the gap. The other men at the meeting Pancho did not

80

know but, listening, he had often caught the name "Marlin" and he had also heard: "Owen might be getting ready to move . . ." and "Got that Marlin up here in a hurry, didn't he?"

Rick began to add and subtract and the answer he got didn't please him. He decided that the checking-up he was doing was about finished. The men could carry on alone until roundup. He had business in town—including a poker game with Miles Owen.

He said to Pancho, "I notice Dell likes you around, *amigo*."

Pancho's eyes flashed. "She is beautiful, no? And persistent, eh? Rick, do I take your woman?"

Rick laughed. "I have an idea the lady likes a change of scenery now and then. And maybe she thinks I've done her about all the good I can in this business." He added, more seriously, "I'm going to move to town for a while, Pancho. You could spend some of your evenings teaching her Spanish."

"The language of love," Pancho observed, "is the same in all tongues, friend Rick."

"You might also," Rick said, ignoring him, "try to get it over to the lady that I've been seeing Nan Owen."

"That is dangerous, Rick!"

"I have an idea," Rick said. "Besides, it will do two things—turn her to you faster and maybe make her less suspicious of any connection you and I might have had before. Can do?"

"Can try," Pancho answered. He did not sound as if he regretted the assignment.

CHAPTER 7

A HALF-HOUR AFTER RICK LEFT FOR TOWN DELL ASKED
Pancho, the one hand about at the moment, to hitch up
the light buggy. She did not appear to be in a hurry. In
fact, Pancho thought she was working too hard at being
casual about this trip.

"I have a little shopping to do," she explained to him.

Pancho looked politely blank and nodded. "*Si,*" he
said uncertainly. He scratched his head as if he were
searching for a word. "Dinner?" he said finally. He
scratched a little more. "*Señora*—time for dinner?" he
managed at last.

Dell shook her head. Pancho handed her gracefully
into the buggy, lingering a little before he let go of her
hand. Then he stepped smartly to one side and raised his
fingers toward his sombrero. Somehow they stopped at
his lips just as she turned away, but she did not miss the
kiss that he blew gently toward her.

Pancho had been in Dell's mind quite a bit of late. It
was hard for him not to be, since he was in the kitchen a
good deal of the time. He was definitely a handsome
man, though rather small—not much taller than she was.
But always there was the flashing smile and, more
recently, the rather veiled look in his eyes when she
came me into a room. He was excessively polite—the
kiss he had blown at her had been his boldest act.

Resolutely, she put Pancho from her mind as she
hurried the horse toward Riverbend. This might be
foolish, she thought, but then what law prevented her
from going shopping if she wished? And if she
happened to run into Ed Foley, what was wrong with
that? Still, she knew that he would not like it, no matter

82

how subtly she worked it. Ed, she had found long ago, preferred to take the lead. He wanted to think that ideas came from him, not from others.

When she drove into town, Riverbend had settled into the somnambulance between midafternoon and suppertime. Turning the buggy into the livery, she got down and strolled back up the street toward the Mercantile.

In the Mercantile she bought a piece of calico for a kitchen curtain, two spools of thread, and a cooking fork. She lingered over some of the latest fashion books that had come in. It was tempting to stand there and imagine herself clothed in the latest thing from Godey's *Lady's Book.* She turned the pages slowly, in a half-dreaming mood, thinking of what Ed had said about the chance of someday going to Washington. It was all a dream, of course, but a lovely way to occupy a warm afternoon.

Mobbs, the proprietor, came over to her. "Can I order you something, Mrs. Ryan?"

Dell came abruptly from her reverie, aware suddenly that it was growing late. "Not today," she said. She laughed a little. "I can tell better after roundup."

"Can't we all," Mobbs agreed. "Do you think you'll ship a lot this fall, Mrs. Ryan?"

"Since we're so short of hay," she said, "I suppose we'll all ship heavily."

"And that's sure to drive the price down," Mobbs finished cheerlessly.

Dell cared nothing for the price of beef, now or later, Her mind was still filled with the warm, pleasant daydream. As she walked out of the store, carrying her few purchases, the realization came to her that Ed had never bought her a dress. He had given her money for clothing, of course, but that wasn't the same thing. And the absurd notion crossed her mind that Pancho was the type of man who would buy a woman clothes—and the right kind, to be sure. She curbed her thoughts sharply. She had seen the signs with Rick—they were even more definite now. Ed had warned her about letting her emotions govern her. But, she admitted to herself, being in love was such a pleasant pastime.

She walked slowly along the dusty street as if enjoying the late, slanting sunshine. She was not afraid of meeting Rick—she couldn't avoid his finding out about this trip—but she was afraid of not meeting Ed Foley. She could go to his office, she knew, but she dreaded the sharpness of his tongue if she came in without an obvious reason.

At last she saw him, and he waved and came across the street. She was standing not far from the hotel entrance as he removed his hat and bowed to her.

"To what do we owe the pleasure of this visit?" he boomed, and added in a lower voice, "What are you doing in town?"

"I had to talk to you," she said, and for the benefit of a few people near by added more loudly, "I came to do some shopping. Once roundup starts, I'll hardly have time."

They talked in a desultory fashion for a few minutes and then he said, "Take your buggy and start home. I'll meet you at the first tongue of timber."

Dell did as she was told, taking her time since she knew that Foley would not openly ride after her. Shortly after she reached the first tongue of timber which jutted out, near the road to the DR, he appeared from the woods road, apparently having circled around to come in from the east.

"If you wanted to see me," he said, "why didn't you send Dud?"

"Because Rick Marlin sees to it that Dud and the rest of the crew earn their money," she answered sharply. "Do you think I took the risk just for the pleasure of seeing you?"

Foley said more conciliatingly, "I imagine you have reason enough."

She told him of Rick's plans. Foley didn't seem particularly interested until she added, "Dud got a chance the other day and followed Marlin, by the way. He's been meeting that Owen girl and going over their land with her. Not only that, but he let a bunch of Flying M beef into our graze—they're bottled up in a canyon. He's seen to it that the men are kept away from there."

Foley exploded. "You waited all this time to tell me that! Why didn't you come the day you found out?"

"Why?" she asked reasonably. "Do you plan to push the beef back onto Flying M grass, Ed?"

He swore at her softly. "It looks as if Marlin's plan to get some strength to use after roundup might be for Owen's benefit."

"I assumed that," she said.

"Get to Dud some way and have him come in tonight—quietly. And keep your eyes open. If anything happens, get in touch with me at once. Don't wait a week."

She looked at him towering above her on his horse. He was big and solid and competent looking. And she knew how gentle he could be—and how rough he had been of late. "You could be more pleasant. Ed," she said softly. "I'm not a slave to be treated so."

"I've no time now for foolishness," Foley answered brusquely. He wheeled his horse away and then back.

"How does that Mexican act around Marlin?" he asked abruptly.

Dell was nettled and hurt. She said with equal sharpness, "He isn't around Marlin much except when he has to be told something in Spanish."

"That isn't what I want to know!"

Perversely she said, "If you mean do they act as if they knew each other before—not at all. In fact, Marlin acts a little jealous."

Foley spoke coarsely to her and then added as he started off, "Keep away from that Mexican."

Dell drove on, angry with him, angry with the warm lazy sunshine. Her dream had been shattered and, try as she might, she could not bring it back.

At the ranch she found Pancho waiting for her, his face wreathed in smiles. He said, "Supper—*si*!" And he seemed so pleased that some of the anger left her. Pancho ate with her. After supper, she decided to finish her one last chore the easiest way and then forget Ed Foley for the time being.

With an effort, she made it plain to Pancho that he was to ride to Dud and carry him the message she wrote and slipped into an envelope. He was to do it as secretly as possible. She also made it plain, with much less effort, that once the job was done she and Pancho could enjoy an evening before the lighted fireplace since, now, the nights had grown cool.

Pancho was gone for some time, explaining when he returned that the men had moved the line camp and were hard to find and that it was especially difficult to get Dud alone. He explained by gestures, which took a good deal of time, and brought Dell into quite close proximity. He did not think it necessary to explain that he had also made a side trip beforehand into Riverbend where, in the early darkness, he had managed to slip into the hotel and show Rick the note Dell had written. They had changed envelopes, sealed the new one, and Pancho had then ridden for the line camp and Dud.

Rick found Miles back in town and at his usual place at the rear of the saloon late that evening. The place was fuller than usual, but Miles had no more company than he did on a poor night. It had been getting plainer of late that even the hangers-on in the saloon were not staying too close to him.

When Rick sat down, Miles said loudly, "Been busy, Carlson?"

"Busy enough," Rick said, and then dropped his voice to cut beneath the hum of conversation and the clink of chips. He said in Spanish, "I have to talk to you."

Miles nodded. "Ten-dollar limit suits me."

They played for almost two hours and then Rick saw Ed Foley come in and order a drink at the bar. Without asking Miles' permission, Rick signaled Foley over and suggested that he join them. Foley and Miles looked at each other, both politely cold. Miles said finally, "I see no reason why not. Sit in, Foley."

"I'll watch," the editor said briefly. He stretched his long legs and then reached for his pipe. "No newspaperman can afford your kind of stakes."

Rick switched the conversation to another subject. "I was about to ask Owen here about roundup this year. I understand the regular policy has been for everyone to go in together."

"Especially on that open range land," Foley nodded. "And besides, no one has a crew big enough to do everything he should. It pays to pool help. You think it should be different this year?" His eyes stayed sharply

87

on Rick.

It was Rick's turn to stretch his legs. He glanced at his hole-card and at the deuce Miles had flipped to him, and tossed in a chip. "Considering the fact that Owen wants to add the DR to his Flying M and I don't want him to, I thought there might be a little trouble, that's all."

Miles did not look up. His voice was gruff. "Meaning?"

"Meaning," Rick said blandly, "that I've picked an awful lot of DR beef out of Flying M stuff lately. And fixed a lot of cut fence."

Foley laughed. "He's heard all that before, Carlson. Owen always says that he finds a lot of Flying M beef in DR stuff and that he finds plenty of cut fence, too."

"And just the other day I found a fat herd wearing the Flying M bunched back in a canyon of the DR—a grass-fat and water-fat canyon."

Miles' head came up sharply. There was an instant of surprise registered on his face and then it was gone. But it was not Miles' expression that interested Rick; it was Foley's. The editor couldn't avoid showing that he was startled and then puzzled and, finally, obviously suspicious. He recovered himself, however, almost as quickly as Miles had.

Rick thought, So Foley already knows about the beef in the canyon.

Miles said coldly, his eyes moving from Foley to Rick, "I thought maybe when you took over the DR, Carlson, that we might make some sense out of this quarrel. Apparently not."

"Not if things continue as they are," Rick said. "I can't afford it."

"Meaning?" Miles demanded again.

"Meaning," Rick answered flatly, "that we'll let roundup go on like it has before. If that's the custom, I don't want to change it—so soon."

"So soon?" echoed Foley.

Rick's voice was harsh. "But after roundup, the truce is over." He saw Miles drop a card for himself that took the pot, rose and raked in his own chips to cash back, and said, "Where I come from, we play hard. No holds barred."

"This is the last game, then," Miles observed dryly.

"Unless we have time to kill on roundup."

Miles stacked his own chips and began to count them. "Have it your way, Carlson. I never go for a fight but I never side-step one, either."

Foley looked a little excited. "So it's as usual until roundup is over?"

"For me, yes," Miles said.

"Yes," Rick stated flatly. "Don't tell me that's printable news, Foley."

Foley laughed. "No. But it tells me to get busy *after* roundup."

They left it at that, Rick stopping at the bar with Foley long enough to have a drink, Miles walking out into the night.

When he was gone, Foley warned, "You're getting pushy, friend. Is that wise with a man like Owen?"

"I've looked him over," Rick said. "He hasn't got much strength at the Flying M. Just five hands." His lips quirked upward in a cold smile. "I can't afford to push him until after roundup. I want to move a lot of Dell's beef. She's going to need cash to work on. But once the stuff is loaded . . ."

Foley's eyebrows raised. Rick said, "Did you know that Owen is short of water?"

"Everybody knows that."

"And short of hay meadow this year?"

"That, too—every year."

"But hay is cheap now. Dell could buy more than she could feed if she had three times the beef she expects to keep—and not hurt herself."

"Does that give Owen a reason for crowding you?"

Rick nodded. "It gives me a reason for crowding him, too. I hate to see cheap hay go to waste." His voice dropped smoothly. "If Dell and I have a little cash to work with and Owen has more beef than hay, we might relieve him of some of his beef."

Foley finished his drink. "Make him sell low?"

"Sell?" Rich asked. His laugh was harsh and brief. "If there's anything left, we might buy it—at our price."

He set down his glass, nodded to Foley, and strolled into the night. He left the editor gnawing on his cold pipestem.

Rick went to his room in the hotel, lit his lamp, and made a show of undressing before the pulled-down blind. That done, he blew out the lamp, raised the blind, and knelt in shadow where he could watch the saloon. In a few minutes two men came out, took separate ways, and disappeared. One, Rick saw, was his ranch hand, Dud. He followed Dud's movements saw him blend into shadow and not appear on the other side of it. The back of the hotel would be watched, too, he decided.

He left his room and moved softly along the corridor. It took him less than ten minutes to locate the other watcher. The man was standing by the far corner of the livery barn, where he could watch both the rear of the hotel and the alley that ran toward Miles Owen's house.

CHAPTER 8

QUIETLY RICK EASED HIMSELF OUT THE FRONT OF THE hotel. Dud, he knew, was across the street and in no position to see exactly who had come out. He would have to come closer to make sure that it was Rick.

He stayed in shadow and walked slowly and steadily toward the river and Foley's shop. He could hear the soft sounds the other made keeping alongside him, but across the street. It was completely dark near this end of town. Since was late, the saloon was the only place open, and its light had not reach this far.

As he reached Foley's, he deliberately stopped and looked around. Dud was not too handy a trailer, he noticed. He had spotted the man easily as he tried to wriggle back to deeper shadow. Giving no sign, Rick made a quick run across the street and into the doorway of Miles' building. Once there, he bent and worked at the lock of the door as he were trying to pick it. He could hear Dud again, this time coming closer. He stayed bent over until he could almost feel the man breathing down his neck. Then he straightened suddenly, bringing out his gun as he turned and jamming it into the other's midriff.

"Raise 'em!"

"Easy, boss !"

Rick said in great surprise, "What the hell are you doing here?"

Dud's voice made a few stammering sounds and then got himself straightened out. "I dropped into the saloon for a shot. Heard a couple of Flying M men mention your name. Put me on the lookout. I happened to see you come out of the hotel and figured I might help.

91

Those Flying M guys would as soon slice your throat as look at you. I—"

"Good man," Rick said heartily. He drew his gun back. "I had a little idea about looking into Owen's business. You never can tell when such information might come in handy." They both laughed. "But it doesn't look as if I have the right tools with me. It's an expensive lock." He grasped Dud's arm as footsteps sounded from up the street. A quick look and he said, "Marshal making his rounds. We have to get out of here."

"He don't like Owen no more'n the rest of us," Dud said.

"Maybe, but I don't want everyone knowing my business," Rick answered. "Let's get going. I'll tell you. Go up the street like you'd had a couple of drinks too many. I'll cut over to Foley's and try to work back to the hotel up the alley. I don't want the marshal to spot me."

Rick saw Dud stagger as he approached the oncoming law, then Rick cut across the street, around the print shop and into the alley. He followed it up to the cross street where he went eastward, making a wide swing so that he could approach Miles' place from the front and avoid the other watcher. Five minutes later he was inside Mile, house, in the study with the shades pulled. Miles was not in sight. Rick relaxed, humming to himself until Miles appeared, bringing coffee and cups.

"Took you quite a while."

"Two men on me," Rick said.

Miles' eyebrows went up. "So?"

"So it looks as if it's time to move," Rick said. He blew on his coffee as it was handed to him. "If you want me to guess, Foley is getting ready to push."

Miles' smile was sardonic. "You've figured that out then?"

Rick nodded. "It took me a while, didn't it?" He told Miles of Pancho's information and of the note that had come tonight. "Now I'm sure of what I could only guess at earlier—that Dell and Foley worked on me together. And I'll wager that the three who met with the men you fired at that line shack were the marshal and Foley besides Dud."

"For a man who suspects Foley, you certainly made him sound the other way tonight," Miles said. He smiled reluctantly, though there was little humor in it. "You had me feeling as if I really were a heel, Rick. But do you think you fooled Foley?"

"I think he's too smart," Rick admitted. "But I think might have him guessing, and that can give us a little more time. No, I haven't fooled him. I puzzled him some when I threw in that business about your beef in our canyon and that's why I did it, to see if he knew anything."

"I caught it," Miles agreed. "That means someone was watching you. Dud, of course."

"And probably saw me with Nan," Rick added. He had to laugh at that. "For what the information is worth." He told Miles how he had instructed Pancho to get that particular bit of news over to Dell.

"She's a warm-tempered woman when she's aroused," Miles commented. "Don't play too close to the fire, Rick." They were silent a moment, each man busy with his thoughts. Miles got up and poured more coffee. "Anything else you've figured out?"

"Yes," Rick said. "And stop me if I'm wrong. About a year ago, or a little less, someone from home drifted up this way and spotted you as Miles Parker from

93

Arizona."

"Or the marshal got a dodger," Miles said. "I don't know how they found out."

Rick nodded. "So they'd already started moving in on your place, being so handy to the DR. Dell's husband died. Then, suddenly, a gang appears in Arizona and cleans me out—cleans us out, is better. Does anyone here know your finances?"

"They're not hard to find out. I've had my office files raided more than once. Carefully done, of course, but I could tell."

Rick spread his hands. "Then I showed up and they didn't know what to do. But for now they're playing it tight and waiting to see."

"But you're trying to hold them off until after roundup."

"No," Rick said. Miles blinked, and he added, "That's where I'm trying to fool them. I want to make the big gamble. It's a fat pot, Miles, and it isn't stud. They'll have all have cards in the hole and damned little showing. And they about know what we've got. It'll be make or break when we call them."

"You mean swing over to me at roundup? Start an open war?"

"Is there anything else? Foley can play it close and cagey because he holds the cards and can afford to wait. But he's about got you where you can't afford to wait, hasn't he?"

"Yes," Miles admitted. "I'm on my knees right now. But I don't see where it will get us anything to start a fight. Foley has public opinion on his side. Win or lose, he'll still have it."

"Unless," Rick said, "we can get him to start something. If he can be pressured into thinking we might get loose then he'll start it. I've made it so plain that I won't start anything until after roundup that it's obvious I won't wait."

"Foley's caught that one already," Miles agreed. He studied Rick with a faint smile. "You sound sure that Foley is behind this."

"I am now—more all the time," Rick said. "Every little thing adds up not only to Foley's being behind it but Foley's knowing almost every move I make. He actually had a crew poised and ready that first night I came into town. They followed me across on the ferry and as soon as I had the fight here with Higgins—they hit. And Foley was right in the thick of it, leading it. When I got away and got to Dell's, he was smart enough to change his plan of getting rid of me by stringing me, deciding to use me either against you, if that could be done, or to find out exactly where and how you stood."

"He caught a Tartar by the tail," Miles remarked. "I have more solid proof than that, Rick. But we'll let it go for now. Before you get too deep into this, I want to say that I can play it easy and drift along here. I can make a living even if I lose the Flying M."

Rick knew how much of Miles' heart was in the town part of his business. That section was no more than expedience—Miles was a cattleman all the way. He asked "You could drift along under this kind of pressure?"

"Or," Miles said, "I can stake my last dime and gamble by playing it the way they say I'm playing. I think I could buy as many hardcases as Foley can. And then I have a few cards of my own."

"Not many when they know who you are and about the charges against you."

"I've said I could scotch those," Miles reminded him. "I can. That's the least of my worries. And I have my own cards. Do you know who Ed Foley is?"

"He sounds a little like an Easterner."

"Montana country originally. So was Dell. He got into a scrape at college in the East, went home, and married Dell. They set out and had quite a career for themselves all over the country. Then they stumbled onto young Ryan and found that he was set for a ranch out here. Of course Foley wasn't Dell's husband openly—that was part of the game. So she married Ryan and set out. Later Foley showed up with a printing press and a fair bank account. He's a good newspaperman. It's too bad he couldn't just be one." He poured the last of the coffee. "It cost me a lot to learn that. But I hired Pinkerton men—so the information is right."

"Something you can use?"

"It's the kind of thing that's hard to make people believe," Miles granted. "Especially against a man as well liked as Ed Foley. But if Dell should marry, then I'd have her, and a chance to really get at Foley."

Rick looked oddly at him. "I didn't know you played that way."

"I'm telling you what I could do. Or I could play it even smoother. If you married her . . ." He laughed. "Oh, she'd do it, Rick. I've seen her look at you. And, after all, you aren't supposed to live very long."

"No, Foley's just been using me as bait. He may even have the dodger on Pancho and me. He may have had it when I hit town the first time."

"I imagine so," Miles agreed. "The marshal is his man all the way through. So is Dud. So are more than a dozen of the saloon hangers-on."

"We can let my idea ride. Yours isn't so much of a

96

gamble. You even have a chance, I'd say. Do you want to play it that way, Miles?"

"No, I don't. I want to play it in the open—as much as you can be in the open against someone like Ed Foley."

"It's the big gamble—the short end of the odds."

"But a clean soul if we win."

"And if we lose?"

Miles shrugged. "Then we won't have to worry, will we? Nan is taken care of. She can go back to California. There's a fund set up to take care of her. I'll take your gamble Rick." Rick didn't answer, and Miles went on, "There's just one thing. You still might turn Dell our way. She's easily dazzled by the bright lights and she's a plain sucker for a good-looking man. She's changeable as the wind, too I don't see how Foley's made her toe the mark all these years. And I don't think he trusts her too completely. She's afraid of him, I know that. If she once got the idea that she could get away from him—for good—I think she'd take the chance."

"I'm not going to count on he,r Rick said dryly.

"How do we work it, then?"

"I don't know yet," Rick said frankly. "I just know that they hold the top cards and that they have the deck—and can deal off the bottom."

"You'll want me on the roundup, then, if it goes that far?"

"And all the strength you can get—of any kind," Rick said. "I'll want Foley there, too, if I can get him. But if I can goad him into thinking that roundup time is his chance then he's sure to be there."

"He's worked on me too long not to want to be in on the kill," Miles told him.

Rick got up to go. Miles indicated the study window,

closed now, with the shade drawn tightly over it. Rick prepared to crawl through and Miles blew out the lamp. But just before darkness hit, their eyes met. Miles said in a low voice, "How much chance have we, Rick?"

"As much chance as the devil has getting back into heaven," Rick said and, slipping down into the bushes, he turned into the dark.

Ed Foley's office had a storeroom without windows and only one door that opened onto a short rear hallway. With the door shut, only a ventilator carried out the air and smoke. It was a small room and full when three men were in it. There were three now: Foley and the marshal first and, after a time, Dud Curl.

"You fool," Foley said. "He got to Owen, after all."

"I ain't so sure he was going there," Dud grumbled.

"He's not fooling anyone," Foley snapped.

Dud snickered. "Unless it's the Ryan woman. She's been cow-eyed over him." Foley took his pipe out of his mouth and gave Dud an amiable smile. Then it turned cold and Dud swallowed. "Damn it, don't look at me that way."

"Then keep your tongue in your fat head. Now give us your report."

"That Mex—" Dud stopped and looked around. "I could use a drink."

Foley reached into a drawer and brought out a bottle of cheap whiskey. He handed it over, not hiding his contempt. Dud took a long pull and passed the bottle to the marshal, who followed suit. "Get on with it," Foley urged.

"That Mex," Dud said again, "is a pal of Marlin's. And they both know Owen. I heard 'em talking and they called him Miles."

"My God," Foley said contemptuously. "Do I pay you to tell me things like that? What did they say about him?"

Dud looked aggrieved. "Hell, they was talkin' Mex. How would I know what they said?"

Foley let it pass. He asked, "What else have you learned? What about the man I sent to work with you?"

"Ark Smith don't say much. I don't know where he'll stand. That Windy ain't much force one way or another." He grinned. "He handles fence tools good, though."

"I want to know what their plan is!" Foley said hoarsely. For all his usual smoothness and patience, there was something about Curl that exasperated him. "Why am I visited with a jackass for a helper?"

"There ain't no call for that," the marshal objected. "Dud's a good man." He had taken two pulls at the whiskey bottle and in the hot little room sweat beaded his fat cheeks and jowls and ran down into the neck of his shirt. He scowled at Foley. "No call to get riled, Ed. We got this thing sewed up."

"I notice Marlin took you and Tim Higgins at the same time," Foley retorted. "And then he got free of the posse. Also he cleaned out of Arizona and kept ahead of the boys ll the way here. That's not my idea of an easy man to handle. Nor is Owen. Don't be a fool, Hib."

The marshal shrugged and took out his tobacco sack. Foley turned again to Dud. "Well?"

Dud looked sulky and ugly now. "Nothing," he said sullenly. "All Marlin talks about is roundup. He's hoping for a big tally so we can sell heavy. He figures the DR'll need some cash soon. He acts like he owns the place."

"Maybe he does," Foley said sourly, thinking about

99

Dell. "What did Dell tell you when she brought the message tonight?"

Dud looked blank for a moment. "She didn't bring me no message. She sent that Pancho."

Foley started to swear, clamped his lips shut, and said "Are you sure it's the message she gave him to give you?"

"It was her writing and it was in a sealed envelope," Dud said.

Foley looked at him with disgust. But he wasn't thinking of Dud, he was thinking of Dell, taking a chance like that when she should know Pancho's and Rick's relationship. He said despite himself, "How does she treat Pancho?"

"Never noticed," Dud answered. He smirked. "But ain't he a fancy-looking boy when he dudes up in them Mex clothes he brung along!"

Foley was silent while he filled and lighted his pipe When it was going well, he stood up. "I'm riding for the ranch with you, Dud. Get ready. You," he said, turning to the marshal, "go on about your business."

"Hell," Bender protested, "I got them dodgers. All I got to do is arrest 'em. All three. What more you want?"

"You're a fool," Foley told him savagely. "Don't you think Owen is smart enough to have a defense by now? Do you think you'd hold Marlin and that sidekick of his in your two-bit jail? Before you could get extradition paper straightened out, they'd be gone. I'd rather have them where I can watch them than running loose in the hills. And where we get them, they'll be got—for good."

Bender took a final pull at the bottle and jammed his hat on his head. "I'm warning you," he said. "You're giving them too much rope. They'll slip the noose sure

100

as hell."

"Not if you keep your mouth shut and do as I say," Foley told him. He watched the marshal go out, then followed with Dud. Since his horse was at the livery, he borrowed one from the man who had been watching in the alley, and rode through the dark, cooling night toward the DR.

As they neared the ranch he said, "Get to the bunkhouse. If they're all asleep, give me a signal. Now go in easy!"

Dud led his horse the last hundred yards, moving quietly through the dust to muffle the sounds. He unsaddled quickly, turned the animal into the corral, and then slipped through the night to the bunkhouse. Inside, he stopped and let his eyes adjust to the darkness; then he stepped past the bunks, checking. He could hear the breathing of the three men. Pancho, in the last bunk, sounded as if he might have been running in his sleep: his breathing was quick and rapid. As Dud listened, Pancho turned, muttering in Spanish, and flailed out with an arm. Dud ducked back and hastened to the door.

There was light enough to see dimly. He raised his hand and let it drop, then repeated the gesture. Waiting until he saw Foley lead his horse into the yard, he turned and got ready for bed.

"Holy Mother," Pancho whispeded to himself. He reaxed a little as he heard Dud begin to snore. That had been close, too close. If he hadn't heard the muffled footsteps of the men and their horses he would never have made it back to the bunkhouse in time. That woman—a fine woman despite everything—was foolish, though, trying to keep him there so late. She would be glad now that Pancho had had his way and left.

He wondered who the other rider was. Not Rick—he didn't sneak into his own place. Pancho's sharp ears had caught the sound of a door at the ranch house opening and shutting. He lay a little longer, curious, and then got up, throwing off the covers and sliding quietly to the floor. He was fully dressed, even to his boots.

Pancho moved with the litheness of a cat as he slipped across the yard to the house. There was a lighted window on the far side—he could see its yellow glow spilling at the corner very faintly. Her bedroom, he thought, and moved on until he stood at the window. The shade was drawn but there was a gap at one corner, enabling him to get a glimpse of a narrow slice of the room. He could see Dell; she wore a wrapper over her nightgown and her hair was down, loose about her shoulders. A fine, handsome woman, Pancho admitted to himself.

He could see no one else , though the low voices were plain enough, as the window itself was up for the night. The rumble of a man's voice was easily understood. Then the man moved into view and sat down on the bed. It was Ed Foley.

Pancho was not surprised. The conversation interested him more than did the actions of the two. It was plain that they were having a quarrel and that it concerned Rick and himself.

Dell said, "Don't be an idiot, Ed. Don't you think I know what I'm doing?"

"I told you to be nice to Marlin—not the whole crew."

"Jealous?" she mocked.

Foley stood up and glared down at her. "No," he said bluntly. "I know you too well to be jealous of you. The

102

fact is that I don't trust you. Get cow-eyed over a man and there's no telling what you'll do."

"You don't give me credit for much sense, do you, Ed?" She was still calm, still smiling lightly.

"Not when your feelings are involved."

They had been over this a dozen times. "At least I know how to play a rôle once I've started," she retorted. "I don't change my horses in the middle of the ride."

Foley's voice cut at her. "The trouble with you is that you don't know the difference between horses. And there is a difference between love and lust, Dell."

Even from his position outside, Pancho could see her blush. "That was a rotten thing to say!"

"But true," Foley reminded her coldly. "Anything young and passably attractive in trousers—that's all you want."

Her hand licked out, striking his cheek. Foley laughed and took a step backward. His pipe had gone out and now he relighted it. He said, "We aren't getting anywhere with this, Dell. Let's decide how far you're going to carry it." He studied her shrewdly. "Or has that already been decided?"

Her voice was hoarse, her control gone now. "Get out, Ed. Get away before I kill you!" She turned quickly and then back again; she held a gun in her hand.

"You haven't changed," Foley remarked. He got up. "We've been through this before and I suppose we'll go through it again." He started for the door. "There's just one thing, Dell. Don't try to cross me."

"I'm in this as deep as you are, Ed. I'm as greedy as you are. I have no intention of crossing you." She lifted the gun. "Now go!"

Foley reached for the doorknob. "Aye, mistress mine." Mockingly he bowed, opened the door, and left.

Pancho waited a minute and saw Dell move to the bed and drop there, the gun hanging limply from one hand, her head bowed toward the floor.

Then he slipped silently to the front of the house and waited in shadow. Foley came out and made for the trees where he had reined his horse. Pancho debated with himelf. It would be so easy to move up, to give one quick thrust and twist with the knife. And then . . . Pancho hesitated. He didn't know enough of this business yet. Apparently they had a plan which Pancho did not fully understand. It would be better to wait, to learn more from the *señora*. And, he thought, the time for that could be now.

Ed Foley mounted and rode off, totally unaware of how close he had come to death.

Pancho slipped as silently into the house as he had to the door. He catfooted to her room, noting that the light still shone beneath the door. Hand on the latch, he hesitated. Women were moody creatures, he had learned from experience, and he was not too sure how Dell would react. She could, after her quarrel, melt to softness. Or she could turn the other way. Still, one never knew until the chance was taken.

He rapped lightly. "Go away!"

He said the words she had "taught" him. "Eet ees Pancho."

"Go—oh, damn!" The door opened and he blinked into the light. She looked sullen and upset, and a little wary.

"What are you doing here?"

"Back," he said. He pointed to her. "Say me back." He hoped she could remember that he did not know English. Talking this way was hard work.

"I told you to come back?" Dell shook her head as if

she were dazed. Pancho could not tell what she was thinking. But he ventured, "Trouble, Señorita?"

Dell made a bitter, laughing sound. "Come in, Pancho." She stepped aside and sat down on the bed again. Pancho shut the door and walked to her. The gun was still in her hand. Gently he took it from her, went to the dresser and laid it on the top.

"Trouble?" he repeated.

"*Si*," she said. She almost smiled. "Why can't we talk to each other? I have a ton of troubles." Pancho looked politely uncomprehending and she spoke swiftly as if that would make him understand. "I could use some advice, too What to do about Rick?"

"*Señor* Rick?" Pancho echoed. He whipped out his knife. "*Si?*"

"No, no." She stood up quickly and put a hand on his arm. "No, he's all right."

Pancho twisted his face into a threatening expression "*Señor* Rick loff?" He stabbed upward with the knife. "Pancho loff!"

"Me? How do I know? Please put that knife away." She pulled at his arm, trying by sign language to tell him to take the knife out of her sight. He did so, watching her with his eyes glittering.

He pointed to her again. "Loff Pancho." He pointed into the distance. "*Señor* Rick—no!"

"Have it your way," she murmured, and began suddenly to cry.

Pancho stood motionless a moment, then he slipped the knife away and drew her beside him on the bed. He brushed her hair with his hand. "Trouble? Pancho—" He fumbled for the word, got it. "Pancho 'elp!"

"I wish you could," she said tearfully.

Pancho took his sleeve and wiped away her tears. Her

eyes were half-closed, her lips parted. Pancho did the sensible thing—he kissed her. It seemed quite satisfactory and so he kissed her again. He would not have relished this particularly except that he knew Rick would not mind it. And besides, was he not doing it for Rick and for himself and Miles? Was he not sacrificing himself? The thought warmed him. It was good to sacrifice oneself to help other men. And since he was doing it for Rick and for Miles, he must do it well. Pancho threw himself into his task.

Soon Dell stopped crying altogether. Pancho's chest was a comforting place to rest an aching head. Dell sighed deeply. Pancho said again, "Trouble? Pancho 'elp," coaxingly.

Like many people, Dell found that talking helped to relieve the pressure. It didn't matter if the listener understood—a listener was all that was needed.

Pancho showed that he did not comprehend but that it did not matter. He found it interesting. "Damn Ed," she said. "I'm—afraid of him now. I guess I always have been afraid of him, but I didn't know it. He's always made me do what he wanted, held out promises of being rich. Riches! What would we do with them here? Ed Foley, senator . . . Ed Foley, territorial governor . . . Ed Foley, this and that . . . Great dreams, and I'm supposed to do most of the work. I'm the one stuck out on this ranch—out with the cows and not even another woman around. What does he expect—an angel?"

She was working herself to a pitch of rage now and she twisted in Pancho's arms. "What does he expect? He leaves me for months at a time! I'm not made of wood! And if I love someone else, that's my affair. He doesn't own me just because—" She broke off, then said, "If I thought Rick had a chance, a single chance,

106

I'd—" She stopped again.

"Pancho 'elp," he offered encouragingly.

"I wish you could," she said, more calmly. "If I thought you could, Pancho She began to cry again. Pancho, holding her, caught a muffled, ". . . but nobody can. You don't beat Ed Foley. No one beats Ed Foley."

The door burst open and Pancho leaped up, swinging around. Foley stood in the doorway, a gun in his hand. He swore violently in surprise and lifted the gun.

Pancho made a sidewise dive, knocking Dell from the bed to the floor on the other side. He tumbled after her as the gun roared. The bullet smacked into the wall just above their heads. Pancho rolled again, reaching for his knife and at the same time pushing Dell under the bed.

Foley moved on into the room, carefully, like a man stalking his prey. Pancho reached the foot of the bed, bobbed up suddenly and then down. The gun flash was an instant late. Lead dug a trench across the foot of the wooden bed. And before it could sound again, before Foley could get into position, Pancho was standing upright. His arm whipped up, the knife sighed through the air. There was a curse of amazement this time, then the gun thudded to the floor.

CHAPTER 9

FOR A MOMENT FOLEY LOOKED AT HIS HAND, AT THE knife slash across it, and then he lifted his head and charged at the oncoming Pancho. His left hand swung out like a great pile driver, but Pancho ducked, striking a stinging blow at Foley's middle as he went by. He reached the gun, grabbed it, and turned.

Foley swung to meet him and stopped. The gun was

steady, not wavering a hair. Pancho called, "*Señorita!*"

Dell walked to the dresser and picked up her own gun. She looked from Pancho to Foley, and Pancho knew that the balance was very fine. She had a choice to make. Whichever way she went, she could not turn back.

"Well, Ed, where do I stand now?"

Foley was busily wrapping a handkerchief around his hand. He knotted it with his teeth and looked from her to Pancho. "It's your decision." He nodded in understanding. "Make it a good one, Dell."

"I won't stay here," she said. "I'm sick of this place. I won't be on the short end all the time. What do you expect from me? If you want—"

"Shut up!" he ordered sharply.

"He doesn't understand English."

Foley laughed. He looked at Pancho and then at Dell's disarray and threw back his head and laughed. The fact that two guns were on him seemed to make no difference it all. "Dell, you're an idiot! He speaks English about as well as you do."

Pancho saw that there was no point in hiding his light any longer. He said, "How did you know, *Señor* Foley? How did you find that out?"

Foley stopped laughing and the look he turned on Pancho was level and cold. "It's true, isn't it?"

Pancho's smile was equally icy. "It could not be because your men went to Arizona and burned out the Lazy M, could it?"

"I don't know what you're talking about," Foley said.

Pancho shot a quick glance at Dell and he knew that the disclosure had made up her mind for her. He said, "I beg your pardon for fooling you, *Señorita,* but all is fair—in war and love."

108

"Which was this?" she demanded.

"Both," Pancho answered. "Drop that gun, please *Señorita*."

"Don't be a fool, Dell." Foley argued. "If you do, we haven't got a chance."

"If she does not, I will shoot you, *Señor* Foley. If she does not turn and put the gun on the dresser and then walk to the bed, I will shoot you. I count to ten. One . . . two . . . three . . ."

Foley capitulated. "Do it, Dell. This is his round."

She turned and walked slowly to the dresser and laid the gun down. Then she walked with the same slowness toward the bed and sat down. Now she smiled, almost as if she were enjoying the sight of Ed Foley in this position.

"*Gracias*," Pancho said politely. He smiled at Foley again. "You do not know what I am talking about? I have heard better things of you than that, *Señor* Foley. Do not pretend to be such a fool. You are not a fool. I am not a fool."

"I'm aware of that," Foley said dryly. "But why should I admit anything?"

Pancho lifted the gun a little. "My sister Josefa and her husband Manuel were not given a chance to get out. The men knew they were in the house—they had them tied up. They laughed when they threw the oil on the house and struck the match. They laughed when my sister screamed."

Dell whispered, "I didn't know!"

"Shut up!" Foley said hoarsely. He looked at Pancho. "Do you think I ordered a thing like that?"

"You sent the men. It is the same thing."

"I don't know what you're talking about," Foley insisted.

Pancho gave him a contemptuous look. His voice was soft and silky and dangerous, "My sister Josefa and her husband Manuel have died—burned to death. Someone must pay for it."

Ed Foley was no coward but now he raised his bandaged hand and wiped the sweat from his forehead. He could feel the cut—not deep but painful—throbbing.

"I think," Pancho said softly, "I will take you both away from here. Far away—for some time."

"Don't be a fool," Foley told him. "You can't get away with that."

Pancho gave a broad shrug. "It is not foolishness. I—" He stopped as a footfall scraped on the hall floor outside the closed door. He made a move to slide away from the door, but it flew open suddenly, pitching him forward. Foley chopped out with his left arm, catching Pancho beneath the ear and sending him spinning to one side. He dropped the gun as he went, landed on one knee and had a glimpse of Foley going for the gun of Dud Curl standing in the doorway with a .44 pointed at him. Dud's lips were drawn back, showing broken teeth. The pleasure at what he was going to do showed on his heavy features.

Pancho jumped, kicking himself from the floor with a drive of one foot. The gun went off and lead whistled by his head. Then Foley had his gun and was turning. He and Dud were coming around together. Dell, standing by the bed, picked up a pillow and threw it with all her strength.

Pancho was moving again when the pillow unerringly struck the lamp, knocking it to the floor and plunging the room into blackness. There was a brief instant when action seemed suspended while Dud and Foley adjusted themselves to this. Dell's wail sounded almost mocking.

110

"I meant to hit him."

Laughing, Pancho swung behind Dud and out the door, his small body swift and quiet. He wondered if she had fooled Foley. He said softly, *"Gracias, Señorita,"* and shot out the front door; Foley and Dud thudded down the hall after him.

Outside he saw Foley's horse and climbed on. The stirrups were too long and the saddle too wide and deep for him, but he rode knees in and kicked the horse into action. It was a strong animal, he noted, as a powerful thrust of its legs put them behind a row of trees, out of range of the gunshots that blasted the night. Pancho lay low on the horse's neck.

"Ride, *amigo*," he said in Spanish. "Run!"

Rick had finished his breakfast at the hotel, got the small bag he carried on his town trips, and was starting for the liver stable when he met Dell Ryan on the street.

"What are you doing in town?"

"I moved in," she said. She studied him coldly, though it seemed to him that she was under a definite strain. "That Mexican of yours broke into my room last night. Ed Foley happened to come out in time and—"

Rick's smile carried a good deal of cool amusement. "And so you were frightened away." His tone sharpened. "What was Foley doing out there late at night?"

"It wasn't late."

"It was late when I left him at the saloon."

"He came out to talk," she said, apparently unabashed at being caught in a lie. "He had an idea as to how we could go against Owen."

I'll bet he did, Rick thought. He balanced between two desires—one to tell her flatly what he knew, the other to try to play the string out as he had started it. "What happened to Pancho?"

"He got away," she said, and looked for a reaction from him. There was none. Rick merely nodded.

"Did he hurt you?"

"No."

"He left, but you moved to town anyway?"

"He might come back," she pointed out.

She wasn't being very clever, Rick thought, and he wondered what reason Foley had for pulling her into town. He was debating his next move when he heard a heavy, familiar voice. Looking up, he saw Miles bearing down on them on his way to the office. He stopped and tipped his hat to Dell.

"You're looking fresh and pretty. In town on business?"

"She came to stay," Rick explained quickly. "It seems that she had some trouble with that Mexican fellow. Foley arrived at the DR in time to run him off. It frightened Dell into town."

Miles said with a smile, "I've told her that she needs a man to protect her."

Dell looked from one to the other and then beyond them. It was obvious that she sought reinforcements. Rick smiled at Miles and then said in Spanish, "The fat's in the fire. I can feel it."

Miles said to Dell, "Who's going to run your place now?"

"Mr. Carlson, I suppose," she said quickly.

"If you're planning to sell . . ." Miles offered.

"I have first option," Rick said promptly.

"I have no intention of selling until after roundup," she told them.

"When you do . . ." Miles reminded her, and walked

on down the street. Rick, too, tipped his hat, leaving her standing on the board sidewalk, suddenly very much alone.

Rick went down to Foley's office instead of the livery stable, opened the door and walked in. Foley was at the rear, setting type. "What's this I hear about you rescuing fair damsels?" Rick asked.

Foley turned his friendly smile on him. "It seems that Mexican you hired tried to get rough with Dell. We're getting up a posse. The marshal is working on it now. The Mex has a stolen horse, too. We don't want that kind in these parts."

"No," Rick agreed. "I have a feeling that once a few troublemakers are cleared out of Riverbend, it will be a nice quiet place to live in."

Foley shot him a sharp look from beneath his bushy red eyebrows, but Rick's face was guileless. "You want in on the posse?"

"Sure," Rick said. "But who runs the DR with Dell in town? I got the idea she's staying here now."

Foley nodded again. "That seems about the size of it. She's scared silly. So you're needed there."

"Roundup isn't far off," Rick said. "You'll want things quiet and Pancho out of the way before then. We're going to move a lot of beef this time. It looks to me like both DR and Flying M have a big drive."

Rick started for the door, satchel in hand. He flipped a casual hand up. "Thanks for the rescue last night."

Dell was nowhere in sight when he reached the street again. He was just as glad, since he had only one idea on his mind now—to get on Pancho's trail before the posse did. He had an idea that there was more to this hunt than just revenge over Pancho's trying to make love to Dell—which he probably had—or stealing a

113

horse. Rick knew that Pancho was capable of both and very good at either. But the important thing now was to find Pancho and hide him. And then to find what Pancho had learned or said that made him fair game for a manhunt.

He knew that once Pancho was found by the posse there would be no chance to see him. Rick had seen horse thieves tried before. They were strung up first and questions asked afterward.

CHAPTER 10

RICK FOUND THE RANCH AT A STANDSTILL, THE THREE men stood in the corral as if awaiting orders. Rick charged in on his horse, jumped off, and called, "Saddle me a fresh pony and a pack animal." He walked swiftly to the bunkhouse, where he got out of his town clothes and put on his range garb. He was nearly dressed when Ark Smith walked in.

"Going after the Mexican?"

"You've heard?"

"That Dud fellow told us."

"I'm going after him—and I'll keep going until I get him."

"Things like that bother me," Ark Smith said. "Mind if I ride along?"

"Someone has to stay around here."

"Why?" Smith wanted to know. "And even so, let Windy and Dud see that the horse trough is full of water."

Rick stopped and looked the long, gangling man square in the face. He saw pale blue eyes, ringed with crow's-feet, and a wide smile that was not in the least insolent. He said, "Who you working for, Ark?"

"You pay my wages," the man answered.

"All of them?"

Smith showed no offense. "I've been in range wars before, mister. Else I'd be touchy. I only hire out to one side at a time." He leaned out the door and spat. "Usually, I work just for myself."

"Before we start," Rick said. "I might mention that Pancho is a friend of mine." He had a sudden impulse about Smith. It might be wrong, but if not it was worth the chance.

"So I figured. Else I wouldn't ask to go along. I like that Pancho."

"A horse thief—a woman chaser?"

"He mighta borrowed a horse," Ark Smith drawled. "But if there was any chasing, it was fifty-fifty."

"My idea, too," Rick said. "Saddle up."

He went to the corral with his saddlebags and soogans, got a stock of food from the kitchen, gave Windy and Dud orders, and explained briefly that he was going after that so-and-so Pancho. Ark Smith was riding with him.

"What if Owen comes down on us while we're short-handed?" Dud whined.

"Give him the key to the house and ride for town," Rick said disgustedly. "If he didn't attack when Dell was here alone, why would he now?" He saw Ark Smith in the saddle, leading a loaded pack horse, and he took the reins of his own pony, checked the tie that led to the pack horse following behind, and rode out.

They went a good mile in silence, heading eastward along the edge of DR graze. Smith rode alongside shortly and spoke. "I hear Pancho learned English real sudden. Dud heard him talking to Foley."

"Ah," Rick said, "so that's it."

"Part, I imagine." Smith took a chew of tobacco and tucked it in his cheek. He rode in silence a little longer. "If you had to go on the run in this country, where'd you go?"

"The gap," Rick said. "And the posse'll think the same thing."

"It's up to us to get there first," Smith observed. They stepped up their pace. Later he said, "What you fighting Miles Owen for?"

"I'm not." Rick saw Smith nod and then spit dark juice into the dust of the road. "By the way," Rick asked him, "how'd you get to know Foley well enough to have him send you out to me?"

"I drifted in and went to his office. I figure a newspaper office is a good place for a man to find out what's going on. He said there was a job. That's all."

Rick knew he could take it or leave it. They rode on in silence, but Smith's casualness bothered him. He could, after all, be a Foley man playing a smooth game. Rick liked the tall, soft-spoken cowpoke and hated to think so. But then he reminded himself that he liked Foley, too. The man was ingratiating. The fact that he was evidently a thorough scoundrel didn't make him any less likable personally.

It was growing dusk as they hit the edge of the hills leading to the low gap ahead. If there was a posse heading this way, Rick thought, it hadn't got here yet. The sign on the trail wasn't fresh except for the tracks of a single horse that showed a trifle lame in the right front foot. He only hoped that Ark's assumption was right. He claimed to have seen the track in the front yard that morning.

Before they were two miles up the winding hill road,

116

the darkness pressed in, made more intense by the timber. Rick said, "If we're pushing on, we'll have to stop and blow the horses and feed up a little."

"Suits me," Smith agreed. They pulled into a cleared spot, built a small fire by a creek and, while Ark tended to watering the horses, Rick made coffee and heated beans. He had brought some of Dell's bread and a few cold biscuits along and now they ate the biscuits soaked in bean juice and drank the coffee hot and black. Here in the hills a biting chill was in the night air, and the fire felt good to both of them.

When they were done and Ark Smith was working on a new chew, Rick poured the last of the coffee and said, "So you hit town and got a job the same day?"

Smith shook his head. "I spent some time in the Riverbend calaboose. Seems I got drunk my first night and couldn't pay the fine. But the marshal got tired of feeding me and turned me loose. I drifted out and then back. That's when I hit Foley and found the job."

Rick scratched his chin, making a rasping sound. "Learn anything while you were in jail?"

Smith's eyes were sharp over the fire. "Such as?"

Rick said, "Read any dodgers and things when the marshal wasn't around?"

Ark Smith stretched his long legs and spat into the fire. He nodded in apparent approval at the hissing sound. "I read a few. He was a mite careless with his cell locks and his office. I think he wanted me to escape so he could have some excitement. Riverbend gets pretty dead."

Rick rolled a cigarette. "How much have they posted on me and Pancho?"

"Five hundred apiece," Ark Smith said. "Not much."

"The Territory of Arizona didn't put that up."

"No, it seems like the *friends* of the man you killed did."

Rick licked his cigarette paper into place. "Learn anything else?"

Ark Smith chuckled. "We'd better be going, hadn't we?" When the fire was out and they were once more feeling their way up the trail, he said, "Windy is one of Owen's men. He let that slip. Dud belongs to Foley."

"I know," Rick said to both statements. He added, "You learned a lot from a couple of law dodgers, friend."

"I learned some Spanish, too," Ark said easily. "Had a few talks with Pancho."

Rick made no comment. He liked this man and yet he could not help feeling uneasy in his presence. As if Smith was all he said he was, but more too. It was the bit more that Rick figured was bothering him.

It was late when they topped the easy rise into the gap and looked down on the handful of dim lights that marked the saloon and hotel that, plus fewer than a half-dozen houses, made up the town once called Kettle Hollow.

They reined up in front of the saloon and left their horses. It was a small, dingy place of one room, a few scattered tables for poker, and a short bar. A heavy, clean-shaven man with an absolutely bald head was leaning behind the bar and two booted miners were leaning on the front of it. One of them had a heavy black beard. There was no one else in the place.

Rick nodded to the three as they turned to look curiously. "Late to be riding," the bartender observed. He had small eyes, half buried in the fat of his face, and they looked at Rick speculatively but without hostility.

"But not to be drinking," Rick said. "Set up two,

friend." When the liquor was in front of them, Rick remarked, "We saw a lot of tracks coming in. There must be others riding, too." He watched closely, testing them, making sure of them before he spoke too openly.

The bartender lit a cheap cigar and poured two shots for the miners. Now, when he looked at Rick, his face was definitely hostile. "Business of yours?"

Rick could feel the threat, not only from the barman but from the two miners as well. Ark Smith said in his easy drawl, "You started it, I'd say."

"You trying to get a fight, mister?" The man moved a few feet from his previous position and reached beneath the bar.

Ark Smith shook his head. "Just passing through, is all. Looking for a friend. He's riding a horse with a lame right front foot."

"Never check a man's horse," the bartender said.

"Nor a man's credentials," Ark Smith said dryly. "All right, so our friend isn't here." He finished his drink, made a face, and turned toward the door. "But when you don't see him, tell him that there's a posse on the way from Riverbend." He and Rick started for the door.

Rick swung around easily and added, "We might also be looking for a couple of gents called Paco and Barba Negra." Then he started on again with the same casualness that Ark Smith had displayed.

The bartender let whatever was in his hand thud back to its place beneath the bar. He leaned forward. "You!" They looked back. "Try the hotel—he might not be there, too." He and the miners laughed. Rick noticed that the hostility was gone, though all the suspicion was not. As they left, they heard footsteps going out the back.

On the way to the hotel—a short distance along the rotting boardwalk—Rick said, "Good place to know about if a man needs to hide out. Those boys are careful." He explained about Pancho's earlier visit to the place.

"Hideouts probably keep this place going," Ark Smith observed. "I've seen others. Same type of thing, same type of man."

Rick made no comment. They reached the hotel door and turned in. It was nothing but a rambling, two-story log structure with a fancy lobby now going to seed from lack of usage. A dim lamp burned on the desk at the back, and a man was dozing in what had once been an easy chair but now seemed to be mostly wood frame and stuffing. The leather covering had long ago disintegrated into a mass of cracks and holes.

The old man woke when Rick coughed. He rose with an effort, blinking at them. "Dollar a night. Furnish your own blankets."

"Stable for our horses?"

"Out back. Ain't no roof any more but that don't matter."

Getting their horses, they rode around behind the hotel to where a tipsy barn minus a roof, as the man had said, squatted near the dark rear of the hotel. It took only a moment to see that the horse they sought was not among the three stabled there.

"I know the animal," Ark Smith was saying. "It's a roan gelding with a deep chest and one white hind foot. Good horse. These are all crowbait."

Rick said in Spanish, "You know a hell of a lot, *amigo*." He dropped the match he had been holding and put a foot on the glowing end. There was a scrambling sound from above them, on the rack where the hay was stored, and both men stepped into an empty stall, drawing their guns.

"*Gracias a Dios*!" came the voice. "Rick?"

Rick let out his breath. "Pancho!"

In a moment the Mexican was standing beside them, picking bay straws from his clothes. He struck a match and surveyed the two. "Ah, Ark Smeeth," he said. "*Bueno*."

"There's a posse coming from Riverbend," Rick told him. "It seems you tried to make love to the lady of the DR."

Pancho laughed. "It might be that she tried to make love to me."

"And what about the horse you stole?" Ark Smith drawled.

They moved outside but stayed in shadow. Pancho corrected Smith. "Borrowed. I will return him."

"For now," Rick said, "you'll ride him. That posse can't be too far off. Foley acted determined—too determined to wait for daylight."

Pancho disappeared and came back around the barn riding the "borrowed" horse. The others mounted and they all returned to the saloon. Rick said, "Let's go in."

"No time," Smith objected.

"I wouldn't want the bartender to worry that Pancho wasn't still here," Rick said dryly.

Smith smiled a little and all three dismounted and walked inside. It hadn't changed except that a third miner was standing with the other two. The bartender looked up, studied the three who had just entered, and, seemingly satisfied, nodded.

"We're looking for something else now," Rick said easily. "The road we came on might be crowded pretty soon."

The man with the black beard said, "About a half-mile on there's a trail that goes up to the Silver Belle mine. If a man kept on the left forks all the way, he might find himself back west again."

"Horse trail?" Rick inquired.

"Ore wagons make it," the miner said. He turned and spat tobacco juice into a spittoon. "First fork to the left carries to the Belle. Nobody there now but it has a shack a man could spend the night in."

Rick put a gold piece on the counter. "Set a bottle up for these gentlemen," he suggested. "It might get cold tonight."

"Mining's poor right now," the man who had spoken observed. "It could be that a man needing help might want a half-dozen guns on his side."

The bartender was breaking out a fresh bottle of whiskey. "Messages come through here," he said. "It depends on who brings 'em, of course." The suspicion was completely gone now. He set up a glass for himself and filled it and those of the three miners. "Somehow it goes against my grain when I see red beards. Messages from men with red beards or men who side with red-bearded men just don't set right with me."

"If a message comes up this way," Rick told him, "it won't wear a red beard." He paused a moment and then added, "To prove it, it'll say 'Barba Negra' before it does much talking."

He turned and led the way out the door. Silently they got on their horses and headed east out of the gap. They rode slowly until they saw the definite turn-off. Ark Smith held up a hand now and stopped them. "I've heard," he ventured, "that when a man is on the dodge, he covers his tracks. This is hard-packed ground but a good tracker could spot three sets of prints, especially when one is made by a lame horse."

"He's only a little lame," Pancho protested. But he got down and studied the ground. "Here is a deer trail," he said finally. "If the pine needles were to be brushed back once it was crossed . . ."

They led their horses, going carefully along the needle-covered deer trail until they reached a bend that connected with the road to the mine. It was a good hundred yards in from the other road and all three spent time brushing back the disturbed pine needles. It was slow work and the chill of the mountain night had them beating their arms when they finally mounted again. By carefully picking their way through the forest alongside the trail, they managed to get to the horses without disturbing the apparently unused deer track.

They had to go single file in some places after that or take a chance on being whipped by reaching pine and fir branches. The ore wagons, Rick thought, would have small room to spare.

The stars were not an hour from being blotted out by the oncoming daylight when they reached the first fork and bore left. Day was beginning to break when they found the shack, next to a horizontal hole dug in the mountainside. It was a small, mean place inside, but there was an ancient stove to take off the chill and four bunks against the back walls.

Rick staked the horses out of sight up a nearby draw where there was a little grass and a small trickle of water. Ark Smith gathered a supply of scrap wood so that they might not use up the miners' laboriously cut supply, and Pancho got the fire going and started some of the provisions from Rick's saddlebags to sputtering on the stove.

He talked while they ate beans and bacon and drank

123

the strong coffee. The fire thawed them and the food warmed their stomachs, and only what Pancho had to say kept both the others from falling into the bunks as soon as they had eaten.

Pancho described the whole affair, giving an almost word-for-word account of Dell's and Foley's remarks. When he was done, Ark Smith yawned widely and nodded.

"There's more than meets the eye here. But my guess for sure is that Foley sent the crew down that burned you out in Arizona."

Rick told him of the crew of men that had crossed on the ferry shortly after he had that first time. "They trailed me back and missed catching me by a hair," he said. He tossed his cigarette butt into the stove, shut the damper, and went toward the bunk on which he had thrown his blankets. "But the fat's in the fire now," he remarked.

"Foley's not fool enough to think we won't find Pancho and know." He kicked off his boots and took off his gun rig, laying the gun by his pillow. "I, for one, am going to sleep on it."

Smith followed suit. "I only hope no posse disturbs our dreams," he said dryly.

Pancho's only comment was, *"Buenas noches, amigos."* All three of them were asleep before the last sound had died.

When they woke in the afternoon, they ate the last of the provisions, then saddled and headed back to the fork and on up the trail. It wasn't dark yet and they pushed their horses as much as they could to reach the summit and get started down the other side by dark.

A few fairly fresh tracks showed on the road until

they had passed the third fork, but from there no signs were evident, only old ruts and a narrowing trail that kinked up to the summit and then down, always bending westward. It was nearing midnight when they dropped off the last ridge and into the far edge of a small, flat valley,

"Upper end of Flying M," Ark Smith said.

"You learned a lot from reading those dodgers," Rick commented again.

Smith's answer was a grin, barely visible in the darkness. "Where do you go from here?" he asked.

"Flying M," Rick said. "Miles is always a good man to turn to."

"If Miles is there," Pancho remarked.

Reining his horse, Rick stopped them at the last outpost of timber. "Here's my plan. We'll get in touch with Miles and have him take care of Pancho. Then we'll go back to the DR and pretend to be getting ready for roundup."

Ark Smith turned in the saddle and spat a stream of tobacco juice. "You said last night that you were done."

"So I did," Rick admitted. "And I think we're in for it. But I have to have room to move. I can't do it hiding in the hills, *amigo*." He turned to Pancho. "We'll have to hide you out until I can get in touch with Miles." His tone took any edge from his words as he added, "Woman-chasing horse thief."

Pancho's voice was amiable. "Whatever you say, Rick."

Miles Owen stared out of his office window, chewing on a cigar but making no other move. Nan came in, looked worriedly at her father, and walked to where he stood.

"Anything I can do?"

"Sure, honey, you can take a vacation." He saw the hurt look on her face and hastened to add, "I really think a rest will do you good. It's been hot lately and a trip to the coast might be just the thing. How about going down to San Francisco and doing some shopping?"

"A little trip that will keep me away for at least three months," Nan retorted. "Just because we're in trouble doesn't mean that I'm supposed to run and hide! I want to help!" She sat down on the edge of the desk and regarded him broodingly. "I think Rick will help us now—with a clear conscience."

"He's got it figured out," Miles admitted. "I didn't push him—you can't make Rick's decisions for him."

"Nor mine this time," she said promptly. "What's happened that's making things so unsafe around here? It's been quiet enough lately."

"Foley has trumped up a charge on Pancho. That will hurt us if he's caught, and Foley knows it. Besides, my guess is that Pancho learned a little too much for Dell's or Foley's peace of mind." He told her about the accusations against Pancho. "It's all over town, and there's a posse out."

"So that's what the mystery was about," she reflected. In exasperation, she burst out, "And everybody was being careful not to tell me anything!" She looked accusingly at her father. "And you, Miles Owen, what are you going to do? Stand back and stay in this stuffy office and let them get him?" She hopped off the desk and glared at the room. "What are you doing here, anyway? You don't like to live in town any more than I do."

"The business here . . ."

"Barely pays for your poker games now," Nan

finished for him. Suddenly she smiled. "You haven't fooled me, Dad. It's because you think a young lady should have the advantages of town life. What advantages? A few dusty little clerks from the bank and the stores who ask me to a dance on Saturday night or to go to church on Sunday! I'm tired of that kind of advantage. Right now, we both should be out helping Pancho and Rick."

"It's fine to talk about it," Miles said, "but it's too close to open war for you to go out. Rick is pressuring Foley into moving. And once he starts, he won't stop."

Nan brushed the words aside. "Who taught me to ride and shoot?" she demanded. "Who taught me to trail an animal across the desert and through the timber? Why did you and Rick teach me—so I could sit in an office and look prim?"

Miles looked uncomfortably out the window again. "Here comes Rick; he seems in a hurry." He sounded relieved, as if Rick meant reinforcements.

Nan hurried to stand beside him. "And dirty and unshaven," she commented. "He looks more natural, doesn't he?" She grasped Miles by the arm. "I'm helping, you know."

"We'll put it up to Rick. How's that?"

Nan thought of the look in Rick's eyes when he had become aware that she had grown up since the Arizona days; she thought of his attendance on her during the recent rides at the Flying M. "We'll leave it up to Rick," she agreed.

In a few minutes Rick strode into the office without knocking. The rugged planes of his face were sharply etched with weariness. His eyes seemed sunken and dark. The two-day growth of beard on his face made her think of a handsome and rather idealized outlaw. She said, "Pancho . . . ?"

"All right, so far," he answered. Turning to Miles, he added, "He's up in that box canyon on your place, Miles. I put him under that overhang where a spring trickles out so he'll have water. I came to get permission to put him on your place. The whole affair's torn wide open."

"Tell it, Rick," Miles said.

They listened quietly while Rick told the whole story briefly, including the assistance they had received from the men in the gap. When he had finished, he asked, "How much help can we get, Miles?"

"If Foley strikes now, we're done for," Miles said heavily. "He has most of the scum in town and half of the businessmen behind him. He's almost got me believing I'm an ogre. He's done a good job." He paused to choose a fresh cigar and light it. He did so hurriedly, roughly, as if it were a habit and there was no longer any particular pleasure in smoking. "The few ranchers around don't count for much—they've stayed strictly out of things. So Foley has what he can get from the town. We have no more strength than my men at the Flying M and Windy at the DR."

"Add ourselves," Rick suggested, "Pancho and Ark Smith. Smith seems like a handy man to have around. And, for what they're worth, we can get a few from the gap and the old man at the ferry." His laugh was a little sour.

"There are a few in town that haven't much stomach for fighting," Nan put in. "They might stay out of it. And there are some who might be swung over."

Both men turned as if they had forgotten her presence. Rick shook his head. "We'll have to count on those we're sure of. And we'll have to warn them right

128

away. Because if Foley works here as his men did in Arizona, he'll be ruthless."

"That's why I want Nan to go away until it's over," Miles said.

Rick nodded, and Nan burst into protest. Rick paid less attention to her pleas than Miles had. "Your dad's right," he told her. "You'd hinder us, Nan, instead of helping us."

Miles looked relieved. "We left it up to Rick," he reminded her. "A bargain is a bargain."

She appealed to Rick. "I can ride and shoot and track, Rick. What good will I be if I go away?"

"You'll give us peace of mind," he said.

"Then you want me to leave Riverbend so you can fight?"

"That's it," Rick confirmed.

"I'll go," she said reluctantly. She started for the door. "You'll be going to the ranch soon, Dad?"

"Right away," Miles said.

"Then I'll get ready to leave," Nan decided. "The mail coach will be in today. I'll take it for Spokane Falls." She went out quickly.

"That was too easy," Rick said suspiciously.

"Nan knows the meaning of a bargain."

They began to make plans. There were few to make, actually. Miles wanted to draw a good sum of money from the bank and he used Nan's trip to Spokane Falls as an excuse. Ostensibly she would be going on a business deal. His important papers Miles planned to gather together and put away somewhere in a safe place.

Rick suggested the old ferryman. "If we come out alive," he said, "and have to run, we'll want depositions in a place where they can be found. Your house isn't safe."

129

"Hardly. That's what the marshal and Tim Higgins were after when they tried to break in that first night you came."

"This is as bad," Rick pointed out.

It was agreed to get the papers to old John Amos. But they moved slowly, as if it were just another business day, in order to avoid undue suspicion. There were few people left in town, most of them being out on the posse, but those few were as observant as half a hundred.

Rick caught Amos on one of his trips, gave him the papers, and explained the situation briefly. The old man took the thick, wrapped packet and tucked it into some secret place on his person. "Bustin' open, eh? Figured it would pretty soon. What can I do?"

"Stay on your ferry," Rick said. "We may need you."

"Want I should swamp us if Foley gets on?" Amos offered.

"Who said anything about Foley?"

Amos gave an evil grin. "I did. Now git, Marlin. Here comes the mail stage."

The stage eased down the grade and onto the ferry, filling it completely. Nan was the only passenger and Rick stopped by the window a moment to talk.

"This helps Miles and me a lot," he said.

Nan's smile was unnaturally bright. "If anything happens to him, Rick . . ."

"I'll write." He added foolishly, "Where?"

She gave him a Spokane Falls address. "And I won't go any farther," she said vehemently. "Do you think I like being stuck there while things are going on?"

"No," Rick said, "but . . ." Whatever he had planned to say was cut off by the abrupt appearance of water between the dock and the barge. Rick had to make a jump for it. He turned and watched the ferry work slowly across the river Then, mounting his horse, he rode back into town.

He was in time to speak to Miles before the latter rode off for the Flying M. "I'll hang around a while," Rick told him. "I might learn something. And make the wide swing, Miles, in case the posse should be coming back. They might be ugly." They shook hands briefly. Rick added, "Go for Pancho yourself. He doesn't know your men well and there might be a shooting."

"Can do," Miles promised in Spanish; he flicked his hat and put spurs to his big bay gelding. Rick watched him ride off, thinking how much more natural Miles looked in range garb than in the stiff, formal town clothes he had been wearing.

Tying his horse before the hotel, Rick went up to the room he kept, shaved and brushed himself off, and returned to the lobby. The day had gone; the sun was stretching low in the west, and the first supper call had come from downstairs. Rick was nearly finished with his supper in the almost empty dining room when heavy footsteps sounded and he looked up to see the marshal bearing down on him.

Bender looked tired, his paunchy jowls wobbling, his mouth slack with weariness. But he came with one hand or his gun and the other wrapped around a paper.

"You, Marlin!" he shouted so that the handful of diners all looked at Rick. "You're under arrest!"

Rick kicked back his chair—and moved into the aisle, "For what, Marshal?" he asked mildly. "I heard the posse was out—but not after me."

"They will be," Bender said. "I got a warrant here. It charges you with the murder of Tim Higgins, deputy, and it's sworn to by Dud Curl."'

CHAPTER 11

NAN JOUNCED ALONG ON THE SMALL MUDWAGON THAT made the weekly trip from the railpoint at Sprague to Riverbend. She thought her own thoughts, not bothering to look at the desolate, well-known scenery. Her mind was far away—first back in Arizona, then in Riverbend, and finally at the Flying M. She curbed her impatience, knowing that there was little she could do to hurry things.

Four days later she got off the train. It had carried her to Spokane Falls; from there she had taken the little northern railway that ran into Canada, getting off at the railpoint where the Riverbend people always drove their cattle.

She said comfortably to herself, "They told me to leave Riverbend. That was Rick's decision. I did—so my bargain is kept. They didn't tell me I couldn't come back."

She was known where she left the train and it took only a short while for her to rent a room in the hotel, change to the riding clothes she had brought, and see that her other things were stored against her return. Then, attired in well-worn jeans, high-heeled boots, and a man's shirt and vest, she took her war bag and set off for the livery stable. There she rented a stout little black, tied her mackinaw and slicker to the saddle on top of the war bag, and climbed easily into the saddle.

"I'll need him for a while," she told the liveryman.

"Yours till she freezes in July," he said, fingering the deposit she had given him. With a tip of her Stetson brim, Nan rode toward the hills to the west. Once a good distance from town she stopped in the bright morning sunshine and opened her war bag, taking out a holster Rick had made her years before, and put in it the .38 Miles had given her at the same time. With that and the carbine she knew how to handle so well tucked into the rifle boot, she felt fairly secure.

She had left early; now, with the strong pony beneath her, she ate up the miles into the timbered hills. Even at that it was full dark and past when she came down into the gap and stopped at the dimly lighted hotel.

The old man dozing in the lobby roused himself, turned up the lamp to make sure this was no apparition, and said, "Dollar a night, ma'am. Furnish your own blankets. Stable out back."

For all her slimness, Nan found it impossible to conceal the fact that she was a woman, no matter what her garb. "Anywhere here to eat?"

"Saloon down the road. But . . ."

"Thank you," she said. "And here's the dollar." Shouldering the war bag, she went down the dark hallway to the room she had been given. She looked distastefully about, decided that it was as good as sleeping in the forest, and dropped her bag on the bed. After that, she went out to stable her horse. Unsaddling, she took the carbine from the boot, decided against carrying it into the room, and hid it in some old hay. Then she rubbed down the horse, gave him hay and a little grain she found in a rotting bin, and went on up the street to the saloon.

It was not the custom, she knew, for a woman with pretensions to being a lady to go into saloons. For that matter, it was not the custom for one to smoke. Since she did the latter and had a vast curiosity about the former, she pushed open the door and entered calmly.

There were a half-dozen men inside. Some, she

133

thought instantly, had the stamp of prisons on their faces. There wasn't a single one, she felt, that she would trust in a dark corner for five seconds. And yet, when they looked at her she felt nothing in their glances but amazed curiosity.

The heavy-set bartender watched her unblinkingly as she came toward the bar. "Ladies don't come in here, ma'am."

Nan pulled off her hat, letting the lamplight gleam on her hair. "What makes you think I'm a lady?"

Someone snickered down the bar; the bartender, without apparent hurry, lifted a half-filled beer glass and threw the contents into the man's face. He said politely to Nan, "A lady's a lady, ma'am. Clothes and talk don't change the fact."

"It's Miles Owen's kid," someone from the end of the bar said.

Nan hooked an arm over the bar, finding herself barely tall enough to carry off the gesture. She smiled at them all, including the bartender especially. "So I am," she admitted. "And I'm hungry. I just rode in from the railroad."

The smile was like a breath of fresh air in the smoky, sour-mash atmosphere of the room. Those men with hats on removed them. Someone swore a little and was cursed—more violently but sincerely—into silence. The bartender bellowed:

"Jud, you back there! Whomp up a meal for a lady. And hurry, damn it. Your pardon, Miss Owen. A glass of wine? That's a lady's drink."

Nan had never tasted whiskey, though she had come close one day when, thirteen years old, Rick had caught her smuggling a bottle of Miles' best out to the barn. She was tempted to try it now, but she knew better than to push her luck. She had the respect of these men; she wanted to keep it.

"Thank you," she said, "a small glass. I—I hope it won't shock anyone, but I—well, I smoke." Her smile swept the room again, dazzling them all. "I learned when I was a smart-aleck tomboy. Dad doesn't like it, but—"

Three men leaped forward with sacks of tobacco hanging from dirty fingers. "Let me, ma'am," a black-bearded miner offered. Expertly he rolled a cigarette and held it out for her to lick, which she did, thanking him graciously.

The smoke and the wine and the flattery of even these rough men helped overcome the weariness that had grown with her non-stop ride from the railroad. When her meal was served she ate it, despite the fact that she had never tasted such revolting food. Underdone potatoes, fat sowbelly, and beans hard as rocks were topped off with coffee as thick and black as mud, made even muddier by some slightly sour canned milk. But at last she was finished and another admirer had whipped together another equally well-make cigarette for her. She smoked and smiled at them all.

"Thank you very much," she said. "You've all been most kind. I know I don't belong here and you're uncomfortable. Don't let me stop your talk—I've heard cussing before. And—" She paused. "Besides, tonight I had to come. Now I'm glad I did."

Three of them fell over themselves refilling her coffee cup. One man, younger than the rest, made so bold as to point to her gun and say, "That's a mighty fine decoration ma'am."

Nan knew she was being goaded now, and goading meant even greater acceptance—acceptance more on their level .She thought, I'll need all the acceptance I can get. She said "It's no decoration, mister," rose and took a five of heart from a near-by table, stuck it in a splinter in the wall across the room, returned to her seat, drew the .38 and shot five times rapidly. It was the trick Rick had taught her, making her practice until she had wanted to cry from weariness and frustration. Now she silently blessed him for it. The five hearts disappeared, leaving only red edges and the dirt-white of the card's face.

Nan reloaded. The men looked at her with infinitely more respect. "Now I know damn well she's a lady," one of them said fervently.

Nan replaced the gun. "Another bad habit I got when was a tomboy," she said. She sipped the wretched coffee looking around at the bartender and the two men nearest him. She had to take the chance that the right man was in the room. Rick's account of the trip to this place had been brief. She said, "One thing I can't do is grow whiskers. Someone laughed as she rubbed a small hand over he smooth cheek. "But," she went on, "if I could, I'd like a *barba negra*."

The bartender and the two men nearest him and another man far down the bar stopped in mid-air the glasses they were lifting. The other men in the room looked puzzled.

The bartender said, "Miss Owen, how about a game of four-handed pinochle?" He sounded genteel, almost mincing. And, as if the words were a signal, the two men beside him and the one down the bar moved toward a table and sat down. The bartender jerked his head and the others retired, sulky and bewildered, to a distant table to play poker. A drink on the house mollified them somewhat.

The heavily bearded miner who had identified Nan said as he shuffled the deck, "The posse came through here with blood in its eye. That Mexican boy wouldn't a had a chance with them. Said some pretty bad things about him."

"I've known Pancho since I was a little girl, and he's good. The things they said were lies. He knows too much for some people's peace of mind."

"A red-bearded man's peace of mind, maybe," the bartender said, bringing them drinks and wine for Nan.

She smiled her thanks. "Could be," she admitted.

"So it's broke wide open?"

She told them, then, what she had to tell, laying stress on the fact that her father was wronged, misunderstood, and with only a handful of men against Foley's array. "My feeling is that Foley won't dare wait now that he hasn't caught Pancho. He'll trump up some other story and attack the Flying M. My dad needs help."

"Said we'd give it," the bearded miner said. He introduced himself, belatedly, as Carson, the other two as Jones and Brown, and the bartender as Black.

"All very common names." Nan smiled. "Easy to remember."

"All names are common in these parts, Miss," Carson, said. He drained his glass and set it down. "We can count on them three across the room and a couple more who ain't here. That makes eight."

"Nine," the bartender corrected. "I ain't fit for years, but I got a feeling I'm goin' to soon."

Nan's grateful smile thanked them all. "If we can find out how it's going and perhaps come in on surprise . . ."

The oldest man said, "Like a flank attack. We hit the Johnnys once in a guerilla skirmish in Mississippi—"

"General Brown," the bartender said dryly, "you lead

137

this here attack."

"It's settled then," Nan said quickly. "Nine of you and one makes ten." She saw their glances and said stubbornly, "My father chased me away because of the fighting. But I can shoot and ride and—"

"And you're as good a man as any of us," Carson finished gracefully. "I'd be proud to ride with you, Miss Owen."

"The name is Nan," she said, "and how do we find out how it's going down there?"

Carson whistled sharply and the youngish man who had challenged Nan about her gun came over. "You, Dirk," Carson said, "ought to take a run down to Riverbend. We need some ammunition and things afore winter sets in."

"Winter!" Dirk said. "Almighty, Carson, it ain't likely—"

"I said 'winter' and I mean winter. Pull out tonight." And he got up and took Dirk to one side.

Nan tried to swallow a yawn but the effort didn't get past the sharp eyes of her admirers. "You two," the bartender said to the men at her table, "escort the lady to her hotel and see that she ain't disturbed tonight." He bowed to her. "Breakfast'll be in the kitchen, Miss. This place ain't purty by daylight."

Nan went to bed and, despite the lumps in the mattress and the snores from her guardians outside, fell asleep at once and slept until a hammering woke her at six the following morning. She got up, wondering what the day would bring and feeling that, somehow, the news would not be good.

CHAPTER 12

RICK WATCHED HIB BENDER ADVANCE LIKE A ponderous steer, one hand on his gun and the warrant in the other. He thought, "So they finally sprang the trap!" and realized that Foley had struck even faster than he had figured.

Rick said, "You're crazy, and it won't take long for me to prove . . ." He had moved forward and suddenly he stopped, swung a bench up with one foot and drove the end into Bender's bulging stomach, following it with a slashing fist that knocked the man sideways.

Someone in the rear shouted. Rick kicked Bender's gun wrist, saw his gun fly across the floor, leaped over the man, and raced for the doorway. He saw Foley looming large in the lobby. Without slowing, Rick drove a shoulder into the newspaperman, reeling him to one side and off balance, and kept on going to the street. He had the reins and was in the saddle before the few people on the street became aware of what was happening.

Putting spurs to the pony, he rode low, straight up the street, his gun out. Once he fired above a man who started forward. The man ducked back quickly. There were shots from behind him now, but he was weaving the horse and the bullets found nothing but air.

A bull-like voice roared, "Saddle and ride! That's the man that shot Tim Higgins!" That was Foley, showing his teeth now, liking, Rick knew, nothing better than to get heavy force behind him and ride one man down.

The road, Rick realized, was too exposed, and yet it was the quickest way to the Flying M. Still, if he drew the posse there, Foley might hit it, using him as an

139

excuse, and so he swung to his right and aimed for the hills. Momentarily he thought of the settlement at the gap but he knew there wasn't time.

Darkness was closing in fast as he put the swift-running horse into the first foothills and then ducked off along a deer track into the timber.

The darkness helped him and hindered the posse, since he was avoiding them, while many of them, fired by the realization that they had been tricked these last weeks, blundered in anger through the timber. Once, while he pulled his horse off the trail he was following and cut back in a semicircle to gain a better slope of ground, he heard two of them going by not ten feet away. Leaning forward, he put a gentle hand over the muzzle of his hard-breathing horse, though the two men were making so much noise it would have taken more than a horse's nicker to attract them.

Rick recognized the voice of Harley, the hardware man. "Foley's smart figuring that out about Marlin."

The answering rumble Rick identified as belonging to Parks, the bigger of the two clerks at the bank. "A typical kind of trick from Owen, to bring a man in here and then pretend to be fighting him. Knowing Owen, we should have spotted it sooner and—" Their voices faded out and Rick moved on.

He had about decided to work his way into the open and take a chance on reaching Miles when he heard a hail not far ahead of him. He reined the horse back in a thicket and waited, wondering what was happening now. He began to be aware that the darkness he had been thankful for was beginning to hinder him as well. He had circled around them, all right, but apparently some of them had moved too and formed a group dead ahead.

The hail came again, too faint for the words to be intelligible. Slipping off the horse, Rick moved forward through the forest until he was behind the bole of a fat red fir. Ahead there was a clear space and Rick could make out three men on horses. There was no mistaking the size of one—it was Ed Foley.

"Listen," Foley said, "those fools are making enough noise to scare out all the game in Washington Territory. Anyway, this isn't the way to do it. Marlin will have got to the Flying M by now."

"I think we got him boxed," Dud Curl's voice offered. "That lookout on the rise could see anyone breaking out into the flats. He ain't signaled."

Foley sounded irritated. "If he is boxed, let him loose, damn it."

The third voice, which Rick didn't recognize, swore. "You crazy?"

"Like a fox he is," Dud said, and laughed.

"First time I ever heard you use your brains," Foley said to him. "Here it is. Let him get to the Flying M. We'll box in the whole outfit there." He laughed too, a deepbellied chuckle. "It'll save time."

"Ah," the third man said. His horse shied, bringing him from behind Foley, and Rick saw that it was Windy. "Miles' man!" he said bitterly to himself.

"Do I pull the lookout?" Dud asked.

"Nothing that obvious," Foley told him. "Move up behind him—a quick hit with your pistol butt will be enough. He can blame his sore head on Marlin."

"You're one ahead of me," Windy said.

Foley ignored him. "Then," he said, "we pull the rest back into a line as if we were going to sweep the forest here. If Marlin can't get through, he's not worth worrying about."

141

"I'll take the lookout," Dud said.

"You, Windy," Foley said, "start pulling the men back into a line. Take the east—I'll work the west. We'll use this clearing as a center. It's far enough back so there isn't much chance of his being behind us."

There were sounds of horses moving off into the shadow of the timber and then Rick was watching Windy riding straight for him. The man would pass within three feet of the tree, Rick judged. He waited. Windy's horse moved quietly on the fir needles of the narrow trail it was following. Rick drew his gun and stepped into view. His voice was soft and deadly.

"Stop riding right there, friend."

Windy drew rein and then his hands went high. A thin filter of starlight slipped through the trees and touched the lower half of his face. He was grinning around the cold cigarette drooping from his lips.

"Come down," Rick ordered.

Windy got off and pulled his horse into the thicket. He made no effort to go for his gun, though Rick realized that the way he had slipped off his horse had given him a brief second in which he could have drawn and shot, protected by the animal's flank. Still, Rick knew, the policy was to let him get to the Flying M.

"You heard?"

"I heard," Rick agreed. "We'll ride for the Flying M together."

"Sorry," Windy said softly. "I got work to do here."

"Don't push me," Rick told him angrily. "We're through playing games from here on in."

"This is no game," Windy said. "You think so, ride with me a while."

"While you contact the posse?"

Windy's shrug was visible. "Those blundering

142

townsmen couldn't see you if you joined them." He paused a moment and then added, "Listen, if you get to the Flying M, don't stay there. Have Miles set it up to look like the place is alive and then pull back into the hills. Foley's got too many men for him to handle."

The man sounded sincere and yet Rick could not feel secure. He couldn't trust anyone any longer, he thought—unless it was himself or Pancho or Miles. "And let him burn the place out?"

"There's not much to burn," Windy said.

"And after he hits it, then what?" Rick shook his head. "One way or another, Foley has it. If Miles could outfight him, what proof would he have that he still isn't what Foley claims him to be?"

"That," Windy admitted, "is the problem." He stirred. "I have to get riding. Tell Miles that Foley has thirty men and some of 'em are on the fence." His grin came again. "A word of doubt here and there, a complaint about Foley having the rest of us pull the Ryan woman's bread out of the oven for her—that stuff helps, my friend."

"You're playing a dangerous game," Rick said.

"Aren't we all," Windy agreed. "Another message. Tell Ark Smith it's squared. The man he wants is in the calaboose. But once the marshal gets back to town, he'll be let out." He laughed softly. "A little too much whiskey. I put him there for safe-keeping. Tell Ark that."

"What the hell is this?" Rick demanded.

"Listen . . ." Windy murmured. There were the sounds of men coming through the forest. "Ride, Marlin. I've got my work to do."

Rick let him go. He would have to go on a hunch—the hunch that Windy was playing it square and above-board. Moving back to his horse, he got aboard and headed north. Windy was gone when he went across the clearing, but he could hear him crisply passing along Foley's order. Once he heard:

"Lot of extra work to my way of thinking, but that's what the king says, boys."

It was dangerous talk, Rick knew. If the wrong man heard it, he might get proddy. Rick shrugged. It was Windy's business and his way of doing it. He had his own chores to attend to.

He left the forest and crossed a good-sized open pasture without hearing a hail or seeing any sign of the posse. He topped a timberless rise and dropped down into the main valley of the Flying M. The few buildings were huddled together beneath a thick growth of poplar mixed with a few willows and birch that indicated a spring close by. The trouble with Miles' place, Rick knew, was that even this spring was apt, like the rest, to dry up when a man needed it most. He pushed on, seeing no lights, hearing none of the familiar sounds that would come from an occupied ranch even late at night. In the yard he halted. The place appeared deserted.

Leaving the horse before the veranda, Rick walked up the two steps and tried the door. It opened under his hand and he stood still a moment, listening for sounds from inside. The air was heavy and cold in the front room, carrying only the odor of stale tobacco smoke. He went on into the kitchen and touched the stove. It had been out for some time.

Lighting a lamp, he moved through the other two rooms—the bedrooms of Miles and Nan. They were empty. Except for the crude furniture, the place was stripped clean. Exchanging the lamp for a lantern he

144

located on the back porch, Rick went to the bunkhouse and found it bare, too—no blankets, no sign that a crew of men had been living there recently. The barns were empty, the last of the summer hay and grain still there, but nothing else. All gear had been removed.

There was one more check to make and Rick did it quickly. The big wagon and the small one, the only two on the place, were gone. It was clear now—Miles had packed up and left, cleaning out everything he didn't want burned.

Understanding now, he followed straight to the DR. When he reached it, he saw lights burning, though dawn had already come. He rode into the yard openly, saw the front door opening. Then he stopped the hail he had been about to make. The person on the porch was Dell Ryan.

"This is the place you're looking for," she said. "Light down."

Rick left his horse, looped the reins over the rail, and walked carefully forward. She looked much as she always did when on the ranch, wearing her divided skirt, her hair put up out of her way, the sensible boots. But there was something different in her manner, something Rick hadn't noticed before. There was a lightness about her—it was in the carriage of her shoulders, the set of her features. It was, he thought, as if she had thrown aside every care, forgotten everything but the present moment.

She held out her hands. "Come in, pardner." Rick followed wordlessly as Dell led him into the kitchen. Miles Owen was seated there, drinking coffee. Pancho stood at the stove, frying bacon and making griddle-sized flapjacks.

Miles looked up. "We couldn't wait. Figured you'd

guess where we went."

"No," Rick said, "I spent all night tracking you." He told them of the incident in town and the posse's being formed. He said nothing more after that, glancing toward Dell, who was now setting the long table.

"Dell is our hostage," Miles said. "We found her here when we came last night."

"A willing hostage," Dell added.

"You're playing the losing side now," Miles pointed out to her.

She shook her head, smiling a little. "I can always plead capture, can't I?"

"Not if you're burned to death," Rick said brutally.

Dell nodded with no change of expression. "Ed is perfectly capable of it. But I don't think he'll burn this place. He wants it for headquarters."

"When the DR owns the countryside?" Miles asked.

"Yes—then. Ed has big ideas."

Miles nodded and went back to his coffee. Rick said, "I have a message for you, Miles."

They walked together into the parlor. Rick stood before the cold fireplace and faced Miles. "I don't like her being here with us. Foley isn't the kind to let her presence stop him."

"No," Miles agreed. "I told you she might come over to us. He's had his use of her. She knows it and that's why she's here." He smiled at Rick's expression. "I have no notion of trusting her too far, Rick. Now give your message."

He listened while Rick repeated what Windy had to say, apparently satisfied. But when Rick repeated the message meant for Ark Smith, Miles appeared puzzled. There was a clatter from the kitchen as the gong was rung, and in a moment the sounds of hungry men

146

tramping in came clearly to them. Miles went to the door and made a motion, and soon Ark Smith, gangling and yawning, was with them.

Rick gave him the message. Ark's smile faded. "Looks like I got a fast ride to make," he said. "I'll shovel in some grub and coffee and take off."

Neither man questioned him. When he was ready to explain, he would. Miles said, "Windy is on the level, Rick."

Ark was grinning again. "Square as they come, *amigo*."

They all went to breakfast. Miles told briefly how he had ridden straight for Pancho and taken him to the Flying M. Pancho had been squared with the crew of five, none of whom seemed surprised at the things going on.

Miles said to Cowan, the foreman, "Tell the boys what they're up against?" The man nodded. Miles went on, "Foley's got the town riled into a half-baked posse. He's figuring on hitting us direct now."

"Where we ain't," Cowan said comfortably. He swallowed a huge bite of hotcake.

"He'll find that out soon enough," Miles commented. "Then he'll be here. It's cut and run now or ten to one you'll go under. We haven't more than a deuce for a hole card." He looked about him. "Any man that wants to draw his time can do it. Thirty a month and found isn't enough to ask a man to fight for something that's not his."

Cowan took another huge bite and talked around it. "We figure we all got a piece of the Flying M, Miles. We signed up to work for it. This is part of the deal, ain't it?"

"We're not punching cattle now," Miles said.

147

"Roundup ain't over," one of the men put in. "Me, I signed last year after roundup. I ain't got my time in yet, it seems."

Miles got up and left the room. Cowan attacked his coffee, taking huge gulps as if the heat of it had no effect on him. He said, "We're nine and the lady, I reckon she can shoot, too."

"I can help," Dell said. She looked at Rick. "There are some that wouldn't trust me with a gun."

"You'd be safer if you were in town," Rick said.

"This is my ranch," she argued. "The beef carries my initials. I'll fight for it."

"If Foley wins, you get it," Rick said. "What if Miles wins?"

"I don't see how he can," Dell answered; all the men nodded as if it were a foregone conclusion that they were fighting a hopeless battle but still one that had to be fought. "But," she added, "if he does, then I'll sell to him. The place will be in good hands, won't it?"

"She cannot lose," Pancho said, smiling at Rick.

"We'll see," Rick said.

Miles came back. "We haven't got too much time." He nodded as Ark Smith got up and left. "Foley can't push those townsmen too hard. So I'd say they won't hit for the Flying M until tonight or tomorrow. One way or another, by tomorrow afternoon he'll know where we are and swing this way." He glanced about. "This is a nice ranch house but it's no fort. We have to make it one."

"Why defend it?" Rick demanded, "What do we gain?"

Miles had lit a cigar and now he smoked a moment in silence. "What else is there to do?"

"There's some excuse for a man defending his own

148

property," Rick said. "But when he deserts it and occupies the enemy territory, he hasn't got a legal leg to stand on."

"Taking to the hills and hitting them from the back is no better," Miles said. "Not in the eyes of the law."

"No," Rick said. "The only thing is to defend the Flying M. It's yours, isn't it?"

"We couldn't get ready in time," Miles protested.

Rick shrugged. "You can't hold it anyway. But you can gain some time." He looked squarely into Miles' eyes. "Send Dell back to Foley. Let her tell him that you've pulled out and are here. By the time he gets that figured out, you'll be in a better position there."

"And what if she tells him what she's just heard?" Miles asked as if Dell weren't there.

"Then we'll know about her," Rick said.

"You'll just have to take a chance," Dell said. She looked around. "I don't blame Rick. But I'll do it, Miles."

"Seems to me we wasted a lot of time moving stuff," Cowan objected.

"No," Rick said. "The stuff is safe here. If Miles wins, he buys this place, I understand. And Foley isn't quite so likely to burn it."

Miles smoked thoughtfully until his cigar was a bitter butt. He threw it aside, rose and refilled his coffee cup. He sat down again. "Rick is right," he admitted. "We have the legal right to defend the Flying M. But defending this place is tantamount to admitting we've occupied it and are trying to take it by force. That's a form of attack. Let's keep Foley on the attack."

"For the benefit of what law?" Cowan asked.

Miles said, "There's always law about, whether it's visible or not. All right, we go back."

149

By evening, tension was beginning to come to the Flying M. Looking around, Rick had to admit that Miles and the men had done a good job. The place had the look of a fortress—doors and windows barricaded, loopholes provided as if it were Indian warfare ahead. There was one weak spot—should they be forced to retreat, there was no way to get to the horses unseen. They didn't dare leave them in the barn, since that would surely be burned. To put them beside the house was to expose them to bullets. The only feasible place was the thicket of poplar and birch and willow, but to reach that from the house, once firing had started, would be running the gauntlet of death.

"We're eight," Miles said. "Nine if Ark Smith gets back. Foley will have thirty, according to Windy."

Rick nodded. "We can always get help from the gap, I suppose. If we were to send a man out now . . ."

"I'd rather not, unless we have to," Miles said. "I don't hanker to be obliged to too many. And if we were to use them and win, Foley could turn it against us."

From his spot in the tiny attic the voice of Cowan called, "Rider coming!"

They watched as the horseman approached through the descending dusk. Whoever it was came straight from the south, not along the wagon road but over the hill, as if from the forest where Rick had been the night before. The rider did not stop at the house but rode to the back. Rick and Miles hurried in that direction.

It was Ark Smith. Miles, as soon as he recognized him, called out instructions as to the hiding of his horse. Soon Smith came into the house, weariness cutting lines on his face.

"Well?"

Ark went to the stove where the coffee pot simmered gently and poured himself a cup. He sat down with a sigh. "Got my man," he said, "but it was a struggle." He told them sketchily how he had arrived at the jail not ten minutes before the posse and the sheriff returned, shot the lock since Windy had failed to mention where the keys might be, then taken his prisoner—tied in the saddle—up through the woods. Someone in town had tipped off Hib Bender and he had ridden hell-bent with two men.

"Tired as me and my hoss were," Ark drawled, "that bellowing fathead of a marshal was dragging more dust. I got the skunk tucked away in the hills where he can rot until we go get him."

"How'd you know we were here?" Miles wanted to know.

"I was cutting for the DR when I saw the smoke. I figured you'd come back." Ark yawned and stretched his legs. "Glad you did. Now you're defending."

Rick said, "Why all the fuss over a drunk in jail? Because you're Miles' man?"

"I'm my own man," Ark Smith said. He looked from one to the other. "And I can ride, as I should, or I can stay and give you a hand. I'll let you decide when I've said my piece." He blew on his coffee. "I've played my game long enough. I've found what I wanted to know." Looking at Rick, he fumbled deep inside some hidden pocket of his shirt. He drew out a small leather case and tossed it face up on the table.

Rick and Miles both stepped forward. "I should have known," Rick said. "Arizona Ranger."

Ark Smith nodded. "Came up after you, Marlin."

CHAPTER 13

"THAT'S IT," SMITH SAID, TWO CUPS OF COFFEE LATER. "The law is the law but it tries to be fair—at times. There was too much howling from too many strangers about the one you killed. They sent me to get it straight—and to bring you back for trial, if necessary."

"And is it necessary?" Rick wanted to know.

Ark Smith looked around and grinned as he put his identification back in his shirt pocket. "Don't look as if there's much chance, does it? But if you come out whole, I'd say yes. About five hundred head of Lazy M beef has been picked up here and there. It started when a blotted brand was turned up. Those boys weren't out for heavy money down there—they went to kill the Lazy M and then run. So they blotted quick and sloppy and sold for whatever they could get. A half-dozen of our men at the shipping yards picked up the five hundred head in two weeks. They're still working on it."

He grinned at Rick. "Your Territorial taxes paid for something. So the Lazy M can be stocked again after a fashion. It's worth something now."

"That doesn't clear my name," Rick said. "Nor Miles'."

Ark Smith took himself a chew and gnawed on it reflectively. "Miles, I hear, had depositions to burn. I've got your proof tied up in the woods—if it lives."

Rick said quietly, "I don't follow you, Ark."

"The man Windy obliged me by putting into jail is an *hombre* called Sid. He ramrodded the crew that burned you out. And my guess is that Foley won't let him live now that he knows we've got to him. Sid is willing to tell all sorts of things." Ark Smith didn't add how Sid had been made willing. "So I say that for his own protection, we should bring him here."

It was agreed—and done. Together Rick and Ark rode into the gathering dark, found the man trussed beside his tethered horse in a box canyon with an overhang, loaded him into the saddle, and brought him back.

He was sullen, sitting there heavily in the chair. Ark Smith said, "You're safe now for a while, Sid. But another five minutes and you'd be lead heavy."

"What difference does it make?" Sid demanded. "You ain't going to hand me a rose."

"Alive you've always got a chance," Ark Smith pointed out. "Dead, you're not worth a plugged peso. Now," he added, "tell again what you told me. In fact, this time you write it."

Miles hunted about and brought out a stub of pencil and a sheet of soiled but blank paper. Sid, however, it appeared, couldn't write. It was decided that he should dictate and Ark Smith would act as secretary.

"Talk? About what?" Sid objected. "I got nothing to say."

Ark Smith wasted no time arguing. He called out and Pancho came into the room. Smith said, "Here's the head of the crew that burned the Lazy M, Pancho. You might say he burned up Manuel and your sister."

Sid turned a pasty white beneath his stubble of beard. "You're crazier'n hell, Smith. I ain't never been near Arizona." His voice was a fear-thinned croak.

Smith shrugged. "I say you have—Pancho'll take my word for it, I think." He saw Pancho nod, smiled, and turned to Rick and Miles. "Shall we—retire to the other room, gentlemen?"

Wordlessly the three started for the door.

153

They were hardly there when Sid's voice rose frantically. "All right! All right! I'll tell it."

Ark Smith turned unhurriedly. Pancho's knife was out and he was slowly approaching the man. Sid seemed frozen to the chair, his face a sick color, his hands shaking as he held them up as if warding Pancho off.

"Stop, Pancho," Smith said. In Spanish, he added quietly, "His crime will be paid for, *amigo.*"

Pancho stopped where he was, balanced on the balls of his feet as if ready to spring, the knife still naked. Rick and Miles walked back and sat down. Sid began to talk.

Ark Smith recorded it word for word, at times making Sid go back and repeat himself. It was a simple-enough document—to the effect that Sid, hired by Ed Foley, had gone with four men to Arizona, rounded up a crew, and devastated the Lazy M ranch. One of the men, an Arizonan, had started trouble by demanding a bigger cut. They had then used him in letting him be seen by Rick. After that it was easy enough to set up the situation where Rick had fought and killed the man. It was a case of self-defense on Rick's part. But if he had failed, Sid had a man ready to fire and get the attacker just to be on the safe side. It was all there—the rustling, the crop burning, the fence cutting, the well polluting, the burning of the house and Manuel and Josefa, though Sid swore he hadn't known about them. At the end of his recital he affixed his cross, it was testified to by Miles Owen, Cowan, the foreman, and Ark Smith, Arizona Ranger. Smith presented it to Rick, who folded it carefully away on his person.

"Our thanks to you," he told Smith. "If you ride up through the gap and down the other side, you'll hit the railroad to Spokane Falls."

"Meaning I'm no longer needed," Smith drawled. He went to the stove, spit out his quid, and decided on another cup of coffee.

"You're needed, man," Miles assured him. "But no one's asking you to risk your neck more than you already have. You've a job to do for the Arizona Rangers, not the Flying M ranch. You've done your work here."

"No," Smith disagreed. "I came to bring back Rick Marlin and what evidence I could gather. The evidence," he continued, pointing to the chair, "is easy enough to take. Marlin might be a different story."

"I'm going as soon as this is over," Rick said. "I'll show up."

"And I trust you to," Ark Smith agreed. "But my orders are to bring you—and not in a coffin. I'm afraid I'll have to stay."

Miles said, "Go with him now, Rick."

Ark Smith shook his head. "No—for two reasons. One, the gap being what it is, no lawman could get through there herding two prisoners. Second, I doubt if we'll have time enough to saddle and ride. My guess is that Foley'll swing this way to hit us."

"Then Dell didn't do as we told her Rick said.

"I don't know about that," Ark commented. "But it's no thunderstorm I hear."

They listened and all caught the sound he meant—a thundering of hoofs on hard ground, coming closer as it swelled in volume, rising rapidly toward a crescendo that could only end in gunfire. It would not be long.

"Dell crossed us," Miles said. "But to have it tonight is better than waiting."

Maybe she thought so, too," Rick observed dryly. At that moment the hail came from the lookout in the attic.

155

Every man moved to his position. Ark Smith spent a minute tying Sid to the chair in which he sat; then he roped the chair to a pair of clothes hooks in the wall in such a way that if Sid tried to move, he would strangle himself. It was a neat arrangement and an effective one.

The sounds came on. From the attic Cowan called, "I'd say two dozen or better. They're fanning out—stopping—one coming on." A little later his voice came again, "White flag out here."

"I'll take it, Miles," Rick offered.

"It's my right," Miles said, stepping to the porch.

Rick went with him. "It's mine, too," he said.

The man was Ed Foley. He sat his horse well, hulking huge in the darkness. His usual booming voice was cut low. "I came for Marlin," he said.

"On whose authority?" Miles asked.

"Bender's. We're all deputized. He's wanted for murder. Care to see the warrant?"

"You won't get Marlin, Foley."

"Dead or alive," Foley said. "It's all the same to the law."

"And if we give him to you?"

"Why," Foley said, "then we go back and try him."

Rick laughed shortly. "On Bender's say-so, Foley—or on yours, maybe."

"It doesn't matter," Miles said. "Foley wants the Flying M. Your trial would have no real meaning. If you went, he'd think of another excuse to attack us here."

"You misjudge me, Owen," Foley objected.

"The friend of the oppressed," Miles said dryly to him. "You have the town on your side, no doubt."

"The righteous indignation of the citizenry, is aroused," Foley said with equal dryness. "Coming, Marlin?"

156

"I'll come with him," Miles said. "I have a few words that the aroused citizenry might want to hear."

"Such as—?" Foley mocked.

"Such as that the man they are listening to has a reputation that stretches from Montana to New York and back again. I don't think that's the kind of man they'd want to keep listening to, do you?"

"Do you have proof, Owen? It takes a lot of proof to back up something that vague."

"I have proof," Miles answered.

"You did," Foley corrected. "But Windy isn't with us any more. He talked a little too much."

"You've cooked yourself, then, Foley," Miles said. "Killing a Pinkerton man is asking for your own death. You should know that."

"I killed no one," Foley retorted. "Windy is in jail—there's some more information I want from him." But his voice had lost some of its assurance. "So you put Pinkerton's on me, Owen. I underestimated you."

Miles laughed. "Go about your business, Foley. You're through in any decent community."

"You give no mercy. You get none," Foley cried. He wheeled his horse and raced back into the dark. They could hear his great voice booming, "Owen told us to come and get Marlin if we wanted him."

As they went inside, Miles said, "We shook him. He knows he's done now unless he destroys us."

"Then," Rick said, "he can still win. We can't. Foley was right; it takes a lot of evidence, Miles."

The first charge was cautious, a ring of men circling at a distance and sniping. These men, Rick thought, would be the townsmen, not hired gunhands. The majority would be simply businessmen, emotionally wrought-up by Ed Foley. Rick said as much to Miles

157

Owen.

They looked bleakly at each other. "How do we see which ones to shoot and which not to?" Miles asked.

Ark Smith moved alongside them. "Might mention Windy did his work well. There were a few ready to listen. I'll wager there aren't three or four town men out there—unless you call the saloon scum town men."

"Then where did he get two dozen roughs?" Rick demanded.

"A load came across on the ferry while I was in town," Smith answered. "Foley's too smart to depend on the weakest link in his chain."

"Then, by God!" Miles cried, and shot a man out of the saddle.

There was a whoop from outside, a sudden spurring forward, and lead drummed savagely on the side of the house.

Rick was sure a few dropped back as the answering fire cut savagely at the invaders. The three or four townsmen, he thought—and drew a bead on a man riding, swinging a pitch torch.

The darkness had its advantages and before long Cowan called down to report that the attackers had pulled in behind the barn and bunkhouse. "They're close enough to work now," he warned.

Rick got up and walked to the kitchen. He picked up stove wood, wrapped an old towel about it, and doused the towel with kerosene. Then he started for the back door, touching Pancho on the shoulder as he passed.

"Cover me," he said, and eased himself outside.

Carefully Rick went forward, taking advantage of every deepness of shadow, of every night sound to move an extra few feet. The wood in one hand, his gun in the other, he slipped through the darkness, making a foot, two feet, then stopping and flattening himself to the ground.

The barn loomed ahead, a dark bulk in the blackness, identifiable by its odors. Rick saw that the doors were closed. His one chance now would be to light the torch and pitch it through the hay-loading hole up above. Once it struck the dry hay no one could stop the fire. And once the light flared up, he would be a perfect target for whoever was watching.

Now he was within ten feet, within pitching distance. He pulled a match from his pocket, held it in readiness. The air was breathlessly still. There seemed to be no sound, no motion; it was as if life had died completely.

And then an eruption of firing broke out. Rick flattened himself, twisted to look. From the bunkhouse, from the sides of the barn, from the corral, lead whined to smash against the house. A group of men swarmed into hearing, rushing the house, evidently running low.

Rick waited no longer. He was cut off as it was. They were between him and the house now. His match flared, caught the soaked rag. Light leaped up. Rick stepped back and threw. The flaming torch arced up, seemed to poise, and then dived through the hole above the closed doors.

Guns opened up, aiming at the spot where Rick stood.

Rick felt the lead whisper by him and then something struck like hot flame, catching his left arm and spinning him, flattening him to the ground. Bullets made the dirt dance about him and he was rolling, fighting the breath-killing pain in his shoulder and twisting to escape the hail of death that poured at him.

He brought himself up against the barn door with a jolt and lay there, gasping for breath. The firing had ceased. There was a shout from somewhere in the barn,

159

"Fire!" and he knew that chore was done.

He got to one knee, drawing his .44 and squinting through the dark toward the house. He saw a torch come aflame there and knew that the attackers had reached the house itself. Steadying himself against the driving pain in his shoulder, he fired at the torchbearer, saw him spin and go down. The torch was lifted again but now the men inside had seen it and a withering fire from the attic drove the men back, leaving three writhing on the ground.

There was a way clear to the rear now, Rick thought. If he could make it before the barn blazed too high . . .

He started out, digging like a sprinter, weaving as he ran. Someone shot at him, missed. From ahead a gun blossomed and he answered it with his own. The gun did not fire again. From above they were raking the yard with a deadly fire, giving him a blanket of lead as some protection. The door loomed ahead, opened suddenly; and he pitched in, stumbled, rolled over and did not get up.

It was an unequal fight. Even after the barn burst into flame, even after the handful of townsmen had retreated back to Riverbend, appalled at the savagery of this attack, the odds were heavily with Ed Foley. Gathering them behind the bunk-house, he counted his men. There were eighteen left. Two lay wounded, three were dead.

"We've got to fire the place," he announced. "It's the only way unless we besiege it—and Owen is smart enough to have provisions for a month in there."

"Tried firing it," Dud said. He showed a bleeding hand. "Them upstairs can see like cats in the dark."

"We'll rush the front," Foley said. "Three go in from the rear with the torch. This time, if we make enough noise out front, they won't think of the back." He detailed them about, sending the marshal with Dud and another man to the rear. The rest, strung out in a line, were ready to swing and circle and come into the open at the front corner.

Hib Bender obviously did not like his assignment. "Listen, Ed," he said, "them townsmen went back. Maybe theyll let that fast talker out of jail. If they do . . ."

Foley was not a man to make mistakes, and his own self-irritation rose now and blasted scornfully at the marshal. But in a moment he called to Dud, replacing him with a man from his own crew.

"Listen," he said, "hit for town. That Windy is a Pinkerton man. Get him out of there! Get him to a place where we can kill him. I want to make it look like Owen had a hand in it."

"Can do," Dud said, and rode into the darkness.

"Now! " Foley cried. "Hit 'em!"

Inside the house, the attack took every man to the front except Pancho. A cigarette dangling from his lips, he squinted over his rifle through his loophole. Each shot was, he prayed, going into one of those who had burned Josefa and Manuel. Pancho shot carefully and with deadly accuracy. His eyes were alert to every shadow, every change in the darkness outside.

Ark Smith finished bandaging Rick in the kitchen, gave him a second shot of whiskey, and hurried to the front at the cry of, "Attack here!" Rick stood shakily, feeling the shock wear off. His wound wasn't serious but it was painful and bled heavily. He was starting for the door to help when Pancho's voice turned him.

"Coming softly back here," Pancho said.

Rick slipped to the pantry where Pancho was stationed. At first he could see nothing, but after a

161

moment he made them out—three quietly advancing shadows, one behind the other. "Coming to fire the place again," he whispered.

"*Si,*" Pancho agreed. "They cannot get to us otherwise."

"Get your rifle ready," Rick said. "I'll light a lamp and set it before the door. When I give the signal, I'll jerk the door open. You'll have light enough, then."

"I have now," Pancho said evenly. "But I want none to escape."

Rick lighted a lamp and set it by the door. Then, with a quick jerk, he flung the door open, letting light stream into the yard to frame the three men. They were crouched, one with a match in his hand, the other two with guns ready. They had no chance. Pancho's rifle spoke as Rick stepped into the doorway and fired with his .44. The rifle spoke again and the three men turned, spun, and dropped. One of them, the fattest, seemed to collapse like a balloon. He lay there, crying like a baby.

"It is the marshal," Pancho said. He fired again and Bender made no further outcry.

The attack from the front produced unexpected results. The firing from inside was stilled to an occasional blast. Closing the door, Rick hurried toward the parlor; he found Miles standing in the middle of the floor, looking bewilderedly about him.

"They hit and ran," he said. "Hit and ran again. Then they faded and haven't come back. Why did they come in like that with the yard lighted by the barn?"

Rick told him about the attempt to fire the house. "Foley will have a new trick A cry from above cut him off short.

"Fire!" Cowan yelled.

One man had reached the edge of the house. Now,

162

through the cracks in the boarded windows, Rick could see flames crawling up the wall. They had succeeded despite everything.

"Do we roast or run?" Ark Smith drawled, coming forward. He loaded his .44 and holstered it.

"Pancho and I will cover while you hit for the trees," Rick suggested. "Hurry before the fire lights that section of the yard, too."

"No one covers," Miles said. "We'll go together or not at all."

"Give me a minute to untie my prize," Ark Smith said, and headed for the kitchen. A call brought three men from the attic. They stretched, standing erect for the first time since they had gone upstairs. Then, feeling the heat of the fire, they bunched at the rear door, Smith holding Sid by a rope about the neck.

"One balk, *amigo*," he said. "and this noose tightens itself."

Sid assured him that he had no intention of balking. Lights out, the door was flung open, and they streamed into the dark, each man with his gun ready. They had made half the distance when a shout arose; then a withering fire slashed into the darkness about them. They ran on, firing back. One man stumbled and another hooked an arm under him and dragged, then both went down. Miles stopped, bent, rose.

"Too late," he said shortly. A bullet whipped at his hat, another brought a sudden shrill yelp from Pancho, who stumbled but regained his balance, and then the sheltering trees were about them.

"To the far line shack," Miles ordered, and swung into the saddle.

It took only a minute. Yet before they could break from the cover, the roof of the house caught, sending

163

light streaming high into the air. At the same time Foley led a charge into the trees, his great voice rising above the noise.

It was every man for himself in the swirling battle that followed. Riding with caution, his left arm in a sling improvised by Ark, Rick swirled his horse toward an opening. He emptied his gun at a man closing in, heard a bullet whisper the promise of death by his ear, and then clubbed with his gun butt and made his way through the timber out into the open. Stretched over the horse's neck, he dug his heels into the animal's flanks.

He knew where the line shack was, but he turned instead for town. The thought of Windy was on his mind and he knew Foley well enough to be sure that Windy would have little chance of survival now.

In the darkness at the edge of town Rick dropped from his saddle and followed the alley that led to Miles' place. There were few lights in town—it was later than the first time he had slipped in.

At Miles' carriage house he tied the horse and then slipped along the alley to the rear of the jail. There was one cell with a light on—otherwise, the place was thick in darkness.

Rick eased himself to the window, stood on tiptoe, and peered inside. The cell was empty, the door stood wide. Windy had got out, he thought, and then he saw the torn bunk, the broken dishes on the floor. He had got out, yes, but obviously under protest.

Rick moved away from the lighted window as a noise came from the alley below, by the hotel. He pressed into the shadow, trying to put himself into the place of Ed Foley, to reason where he would have the man taken. He could feel the blood seeping from his wound, feel the weakness working at his knees, and he knew that he needed rest. His mind began to create fantasies. Someone spoke his name, took his gun away, grasped his arm and led him stumbling down the alley. He could not break away. Then he blacked out completely.

When he opened his eyes, Dell Ryan was bending over him. Rick said faintly, "This makes twice, it seems."

"Twice," she agreed. "And you're no lighter than you were. This time I had to drag you up a flight of steps. Lie still!" She worked on him, continuing to talk. "There isn't much time. Dud has Windy. When Foley comes back they'll kill him. You were a fool to come here. I saw you out of the hotel window."

"How do you know about Dud?" he demanded.

"Still suspicious," she murmured. "I saw Dud come into town. I—worked on him—gave him some whiskey, let him paw me—and he told me." Her laugh was bitter. "I even helped him so I'd know where Windy is."

"Where is he?"

"In Miles' house," she said.

Rick struggled to get up. "Wait," she said sharply. "Do you want to open that hole again?"

When he insisted on getting up, she gave him his gun and hat. He said, "Thanks again, Dell. This time I guess it's on the square."

"I couldn't fight Ed before," she said. "I've always been afraid of him. I haven't changed but I can't stomach burning and killing like this."

"What can you do now?" he asked.

"Give you another hand," she said, "and ride out if Miles wins. I'll have money to go then."

"If Ed wins?"

She made a wry face and turned away.

Rick kissed her gently and started for the door.

165

Scooping up her hat, she followed. "Don't be a fool," she said, drowning out his protest. "Dud is drunk, but not that drunk. You couldn't get into the place without me, not with just one good arm."

They walked up the alley. At the carriage house she stopped again. "One more kiss for luck." And when it was done she added, "Win or lose, Rick, it wouldn't matter. We could ride out now and—"

"We could," he said carefully, "but . . ."

Dell smiled ruefully. "It was worth a try." Foley had no mercy for those who went against him. But Dell's hesitation was brief. Somehow the presence of the man beside her, wounded though he was, gave her assurance. She rapped three times, waited, then rapped once more.

There was a moment of waiting, then footsteps sounded on the stairs and approached the door. Dud's voice came cautiously, "Yeh?"

"Dell, Dud. I brought a little something." Her voice was soft with a hint of wheedling.

Then the door came open and Dud stood there, a smirk on his thick features. He held a gun in his hand but suddenly it was gone, knocked upward, and Rick's .44 was jabbed hard into his ribs.

"Don't move, either of you," he warned. He reached up and got Dud's gun and put it into his own holster, using his left hand and feeling the pain hit him. "Now," he said, "up the stairs. You first, Dell. Don't try anything, Dud."

Silently, warily, Dud followed Dell Ryan up the steps. A door was open there but no light showed. Rick kept the gun on Dud's back, ready to shoot if he should try anything.

"Light a lamp," Rick told Dell. "And if you try any tricks, Dud gets a bullet in the spine."

"Go easy," Dud said hastily to her. "Lamp to the left there."

A match flared and then the lamp was lighted. Rick prodded Dud on into the room and had him stand against the far wall, his hands held high. Rick allowed Dell to sit on the bed with her hands held in view. He managed a brief second to give her a short nod. She strove to keep the gratitude from showing—he was protecting her, though she knew it made it more difficult for him.

Windy was across the room roped to a chair, a gag in his mouth. His eyes brightened when he saw Rick though he looked drawn and tired. Rick ordered Dell to release him and when it was done he handed Windy the gun he had taken from Dud.

Windy rubbed his mouth. "Am I glad to see you! These *hombres* tried to starve me to death."

"They won't wait for that," Rick told him. "Foley knows you're a Pinkerton man—he doesn't dare let you live now." At a gasp from Dell, he glanced briefly in her direction. "Foley's about done, Dell. He added, "Not that it helps us much."

Windy nodded; he still sat in the chair where he had been tied, his eyes fixed on Dud. "I've got his record inch by inch ever since he swiped his first corncob pipe over in Montana." He shook his head. "A brilliant man—but somewhere he went wrong."

Dell said nothing. Dud stood with his arms above his head, his face contorted. Rick said, "Windy, you ride out of here. Find a horse and get to Miles. You're no good dead and we're not out of this yet." Either from over-confidence or lightheadedness, he added rashly, "At the far line shack." Dud's eyes glittered suddenly.

Rick said, "You're going with him, Dud."

167

Windy gauged the situation quickly. "Why not come along?"

"I've got a little job to do," Rick answered. He could feel his shoulder aching again and he knew that the ride that distance would put him down—for a time at least. If he could get to the ferry, he could cross the river. There he would have a chance to rest and still be close to town.

Windy nodded. "Now it's my turn to do a little roping and gagging," he announced. Placing the gun on a chair, he took the ropes that had been used on himself and approached Dud. "Turn around."

Dud turned and, as if in desperation, lashed out with one foot, catching Windy across the shins with his heel. Windy howled and swung wildly. Rick's gun blasted instantly, sending Dud spinning into Windy; Dud fell across the chair and came up with the gun he had jerked from Windy, answering Rick's shot. Rick was moving, sweeping Dell off the bed and to safety behind it. "You can't make it, Dud," he said.

Dud had dropped behind a table and his next shot sent the lamp clattering, plunging the room into blackness. Windy, swearing softly and steadily, moved across to the door and kicked it shut. A bullet tore wood from the frame beside him as he dropped to the floor and hugged it.

Rick heard a scraping sound near him. Dell's whispered voice said in his ear, "Draw his fire; empty his gun. I'll get the lamp."

Rick had no time to answer. The whisper, barely louder than their heavy breathing, brought Dud's gun into action. Rick answered the shot, flung himself sideways, and tried to work toward the barricade of the table. He counted the shots as Dud sprayed lead at every

168

sound in the room. There were four—and there could be only one more.

Suddenly the lamp came alight, flickering weakly without a chimney. A last bullet whipped air above it and then Rick leaped, coming over the table and down on Dud's gun hand with his bootheels.

There was a sudden blast of air as the door opened. Dell's shrill "Look out!" spun Rick. He saw Ed Foley plunging through the doorway and he leaped back, away from Dud. Foley's gun came up, lining him in the sights.

Dell cried again, "Now!" and threw herself against Foley's great bulk, knowing that she had made her choice and somehow not caring. Foley's shot plowed into the ceiling. Rick's answering fire clicked on an empty chamber.

"Ride, Windy!" He flung the gun at Foley's face and charged. Foley, swearing at the dim light, shot again, but Dell had a grip on his gun arm and the bullet hit the floor. Dud came from behind the table, catching at Dell with one hand. The other hung limply, dripping blood. Dell jumped aside and managed to throw one bare hand over the lamp flame, snuffing it. Then Rick felt a fist rise and drive against his chest. He slashed back with his gun butt and raised a grunt of pain. Something hammered at his head, driving him to the floor. He heard pounding footsteps, the slam of the front door. Then a foot caught him cruelly beside the ear and blackness engulfed him.

Coming to was a slow, painful process. At first there was dimness, broken by spots of light, which faded to a dull gray curtain. Slowly, images resolved into concrete objects. Rick found himself in a strange, bare room. He

169

was on a bed that held nothing more than a mattress. There was nothing else in the room—no chair, no table. A single, small window, high on the wall, gave a faint light.

Slowly his eyes made out a figure; Dell sat on the foot of the bed. Her hair was disheveled, her dress torn at the shoulder, her face smudged with a bruise growing under one eye. But as she watched his expression clear, she managed a smile.

"Howdy, pardner," she said.

Through stiff lips, Rick grinned back at her. Then he sobered. "Where are we?"

"In the storeroom at Miles' place!" she answered. "Ed took out everything but the cot." She seemed faintly amused. "He shut me in, too, suggesting we console one another."

"I don't see his point," Rick said slowly. "Why not kill me and be done with it?"

"From the way he talked," she said, "he plans to bring you to trial after he's through with the rest of them." She shook her head. "Ed is clever, Rick. He never misses a chance to fool his public. Before he's through, Miles will be dead and Windy as well. The list of crimes you're charged with will be a foot long and the proof unbeatable. I know Ed. The reason you're not in jail now is because he doesn't want it known yet that you're caught."

Rick sat up carefully, testing his shoulder. Outside of a strong thirst and weakness, he felt better than he had for some time. He understood when Dell told him that this was the third day they had been locked up.

"You could have got out," Rick said. "You could have stayed behind the bed and Dud would have sworn you were helping. Or you could have gone with

170

Windy."

"I didn't think of it," she said. "And if I had, I guess I'd have done the same as I did." The look in her eyes made Rick uncomfortable, though he said nothing. She smiled and nodded. "I know. You don't have to pretend any longer. I'm what I am—this doesn't change it."

"You're pretty fine, Dell," he told her. "Only I—"

"I don't ask anything, Rick."

He said briskly, changing the subject, "Has he got to Miles yet?"

"I doubt it," she said. "He sent a crew out but the line shack was empty. He's organizing now. This morning he was in, boasting to me."

They were silent a while. With nothing to do but stare at the fading daylight that came around the edges of the drawn shade, Rick could only lie back and let the strength seep back into his body. When darkness came there was the sound of a key in the door. it swung slowly open.

Rick lay still, as if he were still out. Dud's voice said, "Come on," and Dell went out. The door closed and was locked again.

When the footsteps had receded, Rick got up and jumped to lift the window blind. He found himself staring at boards, which explained why so little light seeped in. Foley was taking few chances.

Before long, footsteps sounded again, the door was unlocked, and Dell came in. She carried a tray with one lighted candle on it. The door was slammed behind her and locked again.

"Ed feeds well," she said, setting the tray on the bed. "He wants us in good shape for later, I guess."

Rick learned that the two meals a day they were allowed were cooked by Dell, under Dud's gun.

Wounded, Dud had been detailed to watch them both. Dell rubbed her mouth with the back of her hand. "He tries to do more than watch, too," she said. "It's hard to play up to him."

Rick found that he was hungry and, though he couldn't eat as much as he would have wished, he did surprisingly well by the beans and beef and coffee. When he was through Dell laid a sack of tobacco on the tray. "I picked his pocket," she said, laughing.

Rick rolled a cigarette, finding to his surprise that he could use both hands. He sucked in the smoke thankfully and then turned to study the tray. He hefted his coffee cup, frowning a little. It was heavy and thick.

"We set the tray outside," Dell explained. "Dud doesn't even show in the doorway." Then, after a pause, she told him, "He was bragging. They cornered Miles and his crew in a canyon. Three men have them boxed. One just rode into town to get the rest. Ed will ride out tonight and finish it."

Rick said, "Then we can't wait." He had been working on an idea and now he broached it. Dell listened doubtfully.

"There isn't much chance."

"It's the only one we have," he said stubbornly.

"We can try," Dell admitted, and split the remaining coffee between them.

She went to the door and stood there, her ear pressed to the panel. Suddenly she nodded. "He's on his way up."

Rick readied himself. Then he drew her to him, an arm about her. The kiss he gave her was friendly. "Here we go," he said.

Dell cried, "Let me go, damn you!" There was a crash as she kicked the now-empty tray across the room. "Get

172

away or I'll kill you!"

"You've fooled me long enough!" Rick shouted. "Go on and yell. Who's going to hear you?"

Dell sobbed; then kicked an empty plate so that it shattered. They didn't hear the key turn in the lock but both of them saw the candle flame flicker and go out as the door was thrown open.

This was it, Rick knew. If Dud exposed himself even for an instant, the trick would have worked. If not—then it was that much wasted effort.

As though neither knew what was taking place by the door, Dell screamed again and threw a cup, shattering it on the wall above Rick's head. He was out of reach of the doorway, but suddenly he staggered across the opening, swearing.

From the corner of his eye he saw Dud, half-crouched, suspicious, but drawn by Dell's frantic screams. Without pausing in his backward stagger, Rick swept his right arm around. The heavy cup crashed full between Dud's eyes. The gun he held went off, the bullet whining down the hallway. Rick caught his balance and followed into the hall. He made a dive for Dud, but there was no need. He was stretched out cold.

"Quick!" Rick ordered Dell.

They dragged Dud into the room, where Rick hooked on his belt and gun, emptied his pockets of the things he thought might be useful, trussed the man with his own belt, and left him on the floor. Then, together, they hurried down the stairs.

When they were outside, standing in deep shadow, they heard the sounds from the main street. They reached the carriage house and peered out, watching as Ed Foley's posse streamed by. Rick counted seventeen and knew that the townsmen had washed their hands of this again.

"Horses?"

"The livery," she whispered, "if they—"

"They will," Rick said, and hurried her that way.

CHAPTER 14

THE LIVERY HAD A DIM LIGHT BURNING AND THE NIGHT hostler was wide awake, talking to Harley, the hardware man, about the posse, when the wild-eyed man with the gun suddenly appeared.

"Marlin!" Harley exclaimed.

Rick said briefly, "They've got Miles Owen and his crew cornered in a canyon. Foley's riding to wipe him out." He gave a brief account of his escape. Dell Ryan appeared beside him and the hardware man blinked in surprise.

The hostler brought two horses. "We're out of this," Harley said. "All I know is that you'll get a fair trial, Marlin. But Foley said—"

Dell cried, "You're believing what Ed wants you to believe. He's made fools of all of you—just as he made a fool of me for six years."

The man shook his head stubbornly. While Rick tested the saddles, Dell said, "What do you think Foley wants—your love? Before he's done, he'll have the whole valley and the town in his power. You'll be taking his orders, paying him tribute." The man's expression didn't change. Rick helped her into the saddle. Dell swung the horse toward the door. "I'm telling you what Ed will do. I know—I'm his wife!"

Rick said, "If there's any life in this town, you'd better get them riding for the Flying M. Or you'll see

174

innocent men shot down."

"The word of an escaped murderer and his woman—" the man began dogmatically. But Rick and Dell were gone, spurring into the alley and up the street. Before they had got out of earshot, they could hear the hue and cry being raised.

Dell rode well, keeping up with him as they pressed along the trail Rick had previously taken through the forest. He did not risk following the posse but cut over into the hills.

"There's only one canyon where they could be boxed in," Dell said as they slowed to take a steep pitch. Rick nodded.

"We're not going there," Rick said surprisingly. "What can one more gun do against that crew?" He thought of the gap and now he told her about it. "There may be some help there. When we reach it, you keep on riding for the rail-road. Even if Foley wins, you're out of the way . . ."

Dell didn't answer. Rick led the way along a ridge, dropped onto a small bare flat and then they were in the timber again. The livery horses slowed and finally they had to let them set their own maddening pace.

The gap, Rick estimated, was a long time off, when he heard a noise like—thunder surging from above. He drew Dell off the trail, into the bushes. A group of ten appeared coming down the trail. A line of crescent moon threw enough light down so that he could make out the members of the party. Rick recognized the heavy bartender, the bearded miners he had talked to, and with them a small, too familiar figure on horseback.

He stepped into the trail. "Nan!"

The group reined up. Dell and Rick started their story hurriedly. Nan glanced at Dell, then said, "We know.

Our man got back from town not an hour ago."

"You can't go on with this," Rick said to her.

The bartender's voice was firm. "Let's ride, friend. And don't tell the lady what she can't do. She's all man, she is."

As they moved down the trail, Rick tried to talk to Nan. She only said, "So you finally won her over, Rick. Your charm is unstoppable." And then the pitch was too steep to do more than guide the horses. Once on a flat, they all bunched up together and Nan gave directions to the canyon.

Rick broke in. "The posse will ring the hole and try to drive them toward the entrance. You won't get anywhere by charging in."

"How would you do it?"

Rick outlined his idea. "They'll have had an hour's start on us but if there's time, this will work." He talked earnestly. They listened intently and finally "General" Brown said dryly, "It's a good idea—if it works. If it don't, we're done for too."

They rode on, moving into the hills, not following any set trails now. Finally a low signal stopped them and they split up, no two men going together. Rick tried to stick with Nan but she shook her head. "It was your idea to split up. We'll stick to it."

She rode off into the darkness. Rick had a few words with Dell and found she had been given a gun by one of the men in the ranks behind. "For a miner, he sweet-talks well," she said lightly, and then was gone.

Rick rode toward the canyon mouth, near where he figured the strength of Foley's force would be. He left his horse in some bushes and walked silently over the needle-covered ground to a rock escarpment and then eased himself slowly up until he could see down into the

176

canyon.

So far, there had been no sound. Below, a fire was going, and Rick could see a shadowy form move out and throw wood on it. The men, he knew, would be under the protection of the rock overhang where he had left Pancho. It was the one safe place in the small, boxed-in gulch. There was water and fuel. As long as food and ammunition held out, they could stay there.

He moved carefully to a new position. At first there was no sound, then he heard a rustle not far below him and he moved deeper into shadow, easing himself in the direction of the noise. The man loomed ahead, picked out by a ray of moonlight. Rick stepped more cautiously, fearful of hitting a small, rolling stone. The other was watching intently, a rifle in the crook of his arm.

Rick moved close and reached, getting his arm about the other man's neck, choking off sound. He brought a knee into the man's back and his free arm whipped around and grasped the rifle. Driving his knee deeper, he bent the man back.

There was a low gurgle. Dropping the rifle, Rick lifted the other's .44 and then released his hold. The man turned, his arms up. Rick recognized one of the saloon hangers-on. He said, "You're done. A crew has moved in from the gap. If you want your hide, start talking. And talk soft!"

"Hell, I don't know nothin', Marlin."

"I'll put a bullet in your belly, then. You can take a long time to die that way."

He let the gun hammer click into place. The man said quickly, "Foley's got this place surrounded. He's blowin' the entrance shut with dynamite. Then when day comes, we'll pick 'em off."

"Where is he?"

"Down to the hole, layin' the dynamite. There's about ten men there. They ain't chancin' a rush out."

Ten, Rick figured. That meant six more at the most on the edge right now. If everyone had got his man as he had . . .

"All right," he said, and drove his gun barrel at the other's temple. The man folded down as another blow caught him behind the ear. Rick caught him, lowered him to the ground, and quickly tied him with his own belt and gagged him with his bandanna. Picking up the rifle, he located extra cartridges and then moved off again, this time upward, toward the prearranged meeting place.

One by one, the men from the gap appeared, most of them carrying a rifle and six-gun as a trophy.

When all but two were there, Rick told them what he had found out. "I want someone to climb down into the canyon with a message," he said.

"I'll take it," Nan said. Stray moonlight highlighted her features. Rick took one look at the set of them and did not argue.

He said, "We'll hit them from two sides as soon as the moon swings up over the hill and hits the canyon mouth. There's about an hour."

The last two stragglers showed up, and Rick split the group in two, half of them riding behind "General" Brown, half behind himself. Dell rode thigh to thigh with him as they slipped off into the dark.

There was a pause, a grouping, a silent waiting where the timber sloped off into the flat bowl of the land that opened out from the canyon's rocky entrance. Rick watched the moonlight, saw it brightening, and then the moon itself moved into a notch in the hills and shed its pale light down on the canyon.

A half-dozen shadowy forms became visible. Two more could be seen on the rocks. Rick guessed that they were planting the dynamite. Then he gave a whoop, and drove his horse down the slope. The others streamed behind him. Those on the far side came into sight, swinging into action.

The men below turned and raced for their horses in the rocks. Guns opened up, catching them in a withering crossfire. They fled for the rocks, shooting as they went, the night now a turmoil of blasting guns and screaming lead. From the canyon mouth a cry rose and horsemen thundered out, firing as they came.

A cloud scudded over the moon and the firing ceased. Rick felt a swirl of horses driving against his mount and he was swept with the tide into the canyon. There someone broke free and galloped for the distant end.

The moon broke through the clouds. Rick saw a face loom beside him, a face he recognized, and he fired. The man went out of the saddle. The fleeing rider turned and fired twice. Rick heard his horse nicker as a bullet scraped his hide. The animal reared and plunged and, out of control, carried Rick for the other rider.

They neared the fire and Rick saw the red hair and beard of Ed Foley, who was riding hatless now. Foley circled his horse around the fire and drove straight for Rick, his gun raised, seeking an opening.

They came together shoulder to shoulder, their horses crashing against each other. Both men pitched from the saddle. Rick rolled as he hit, came up to one knee to see Foley rising hugely out of the night. Foley's gun cracked simultaneously with his own. Foley's bullet whipped at his hat and then he fired again. But there had been no need. Like a great tree crashing, Ed Foley

179

toppled forward, rolled over and lay twitching.

It was past ten in the morning when the procession rode into Riverbend, down the main street, and up to the jail. Some were tied belly-down over saddles—as Ark Smith said, they were fit for nothing but burying. More were wounded and these were given somewhat gentler care. A few had nothing more than bumps on the head, They were hustled unceremoniously into the jail and packed into the two cells.

Ed Foley lay with the other wounded, on the jailhouse porch, while someone went to fetch the doctor. The townspeople crowded around, some of them warily, when finally Miles Owen turned to face them.

"You haven't any marshal," he said in a loud voice. "Hib Bender is out at the Flying M—dead. I suggest you appoint one of your number for the job. There are criminals here to be taken care of."

Pryor, the owner of the grocery store, stepped forward. "We took care of that. This is a citizens' committee and every man here is armed, Owen. You and Marlin and the rest of your crew are under arrest."

Miles shook his head and smiled tiredly. "Don't do anything you'd be sorry for, friend."

"We're only sorry we didn't string you up a danged sight sooner!" Pryor retorted.

It was Windy who pushed Miles aside and stepped forward. He looked down at them coldly, plainly in no mood to humor a crowd at this time. He said levelly, "Miles Owen came into this country and started building it. The rest of you moved in after the labor was done and started getting fat on his sweat. Now you figure he's done everything and you can suck him dry and throw his bones to one side. If I were Miles Owen,

180

I'd say the hell with the lot of you, pull my ranch and my plans out and let you do some sweating and starving on your own for a while."

"Who the hell are you to talk like that?" cried a voice from the crowd.

Windy went on, "I notice that when it got hot, not a one of you went out to help anyone—not Miles Owen nor even Ed Foley, though you believed what he said because it sounded good. Now you come puling to get fat on the leavings." He paused, a sweating little man, glaring in anger down at the equally angry faces raised to him. "I'll tell you who I am—I'm the man that's been warning you against Ed Foley, warning you against believing everything he said. What do you think he wanted you for—your good looks?"

Someone tried to raise a gun, but Harley knocked the arm up. "Well do this peaceable!"

Miles Owen moved back in front. "Your question, friend, is a good one. Who is he? He's a Pinkerton man who's here because he trailed Ed Foley here."

Windy reached into some inner recess of his clothing and brought out a thin sheaf of papers. He unfolded them slowly while the believers gawked at him and the doubters stirred uncomfortably. When he was finished, he had a half-dozen small dodgers, and these he passed down into the crowd.

"That's Ed Foley," he said. "Forger, bigamist, mail robber, and counterfeiter. That's the man that moved in here and stirred you all up against Owen. Now answer this honestly: Did any of you have trouble with Owen until Foley came?"

It was easy after that. No man likes to be made a fool of, and all of them were beginning to realize that Foley had done just that to each of them. And when, finally, the doctor got around to treating Foley, he found him dead. The people dispersed then, going to their homes.

"Funny thing about that," Ark Smith said mildly, as they were eating at Miles' house. "I thought Rick shot him, yet he dies with a knife wound in his chest."

Pancho was busily drinking coffee and whispering to Dell, sitting beside him. There was real satisfaction on his face for the first time since he and Rick had reached Washington Territory. Rick murmured, "*Ojo por ojo, diente por diente.*"

Ark Smith's head jerked up. "Just quoting the Bible, Ark. 'An eye for an eye—!' " Rick pushed his empty plate away and rolled a cigarette. "When are we leaving for Arizona?"

"Soon as I collect Sid from that canyon," Ark replied. "Seems I left there in such a hurry I forgot all about him."

"You're not letting him take you back!" Nan cried to Rick.

"We'll come back, Nan. And all our names will be cleared when we do." Rick got up and walked alone to the front veranda. It was a quiet night, and he was tired after the last brutal days. He felt glad to stand in the coolness and listen to the night sounds. Soon it would be time for roundup. He hoped that he could be back by then.

There was a sound behind him and he turned to see Dell coming through the doorway. She stopped beside him. "I'm off, Rick. Someone is seeing me over to the railroad."

"To where, Dell?"

"To Arizona, if you agree," she said. "Miles traded me—*his* interest in the Lazy M for mine in the DR. I'll get some cash to boot, of course."

"I have no interest in the Lazy M," Rick said. "I was just foreman."

"Miles said you had," she retorted. "But you'll have all you can do up here, won't you, with both places. being put together?" She put a hand on his arm. "Rick, Nan is talking much too sweetly to me. You'd better set her straight." Then, with a low laugh and a warm pressure of her fingers, she was gone, disappearing into the dusk.

Inside the house, Miles and Pancho were having coffee in the study. Miles suggested a game of stud. Pancho said, "*Gracias*, Miles, but I have an engagement." His teeth flashed in a smile. "I like your country, Miles, but I want to go back to Arizona. I think Rick will sell me his part of the Lazy M.

"If you can make him believe he has an interest in it," Miles said. Then he stopped, his cup halfway to his lips. "Wait a minute. Dell Ryan already owns half of it."

"So I know," Pancho agreed. His eyes danced. "And so at last, the Lazy M will have a *señora,* you see. It is all arranged between us."

He set down his cup and started for the door, laughing at Miles' bewilderment. "The lady has forgiven me for making love only in Spanish. I have promised to do it in English until she learns the more beautiful words. Now I must go, *amigo.* There is a wedding at the gap tonight. One of the men was once a sea captain. It will be in the church when we get home of course, but for now—" He shrugged eloquently. "Tell Ark Smith I will wait for him in Tucson. *Adios,* Miles."

"*Adios,*" Miles repeated. It was all he could answer for the moment. And then, as he heard the hoofbeats of Pancho's horse, he aroused himself and ran to where the others were still sitting around the table. The gleam of youth was back in his eyes.

"Get ready to ride!" he ordered. "We're going to the gap tonight."

On the veranda, Rick and Nan were standing close to each other, too absorbed to hear much of the noise from inside. Rick said, "Dell is gone. Nan."

"Are you sorry?"

"No," he admitted. "This isn't her kind of country." He looked down at Nan; her face was upturned questioningly. "She helped—in her way. There at the end, she risked her life for us. But it was still a kind of game to her. She's no one to ride the range with."

Nan laughed a little. "I guess I've been jealous, Rick. When I saw you with her in the hills . . ."

"No call," Rick said. "There's never been any call, Nan. Not since I found out you had got big enough to be called a woman."

"And I loved you from the first day I saw you," she murmured. "You were so blind, Rick!"

"I guess I was," he confessed.

She laughed again and lifted his tobacco sack from his pocket. Deftly she rolled herself a cigarette, making a face at him over the match he reluctantly struck for her. "I won't do it in public, I promise." She moved closer to him and whispered, "Rick, shall we build our house near the river or up in the hills?"

"House!" He paused, then recovered himself. "Nan, are you—proposing?"

"Someone has to," she answered haltingly. "You never will take the initiative with me."

Rick plucked the cigarette from her fingers, dropped it, and put his boot toe over the coal. Then he pulled her into his arms. His kiss left no doubt about initiative.

184

He lifted his head abruptly as the door burst open and Miles and the crew roared noisily onto the porch. "Saddle and ride!" Miles shouted at them. "And bring your guns. We're going to the gap and give that devil Pancho and his bride a charivari that will blow them clean to Arizona."

Nan said mischievously, "Save a little celebration, Dad, for Rick and me. As soon as he gets back, we're going to be . . ."

Rick felt awkward. It was his place, he figured, to make such an announcement. But he could think of only one way to shut her up. He kissed her again, thoroughly. Nan's words faded to a gurgle and then she was silent.

Neither one seemed aware of the fact that the rest rode off without them.

The End

We hope that you enjoyed reading this
Sagebrush Large Print Western.
If you would like to read more Sagebrush titles,
ask your librarian or contact the Publishers:

United States and Canada

Thomas T. Beeler, *Publisher*
Post Office Box 659
Hampton Falls, New Hampshire 03844-0659
(800) 251-8726

United Kingdom, Eire, and
the Republic of South Africa

Isis Publishing Ltd
7 Centremead
Osney Mead
Oxford OX2 0ES England
(01865) 250333

Australia and New Zealand

Australian Large Print Audio & Video P/L
17 Mohr Street
Tullamarine, Victoria, 3043, Australia
1 800 335 364